A CURIOUS CAT WAGS A FISHY TALE

CHIP WEINERT

CHAPTER 1

Here's the Hook

Tkzzzzzzzzzzzzz!" the fishing reel sang as yard after yard of twenty-pound test monofilament screamed off the spool.

"Woooo-hoooo! Fish on!" my friend Trapper yelled while I fought to hold on to both my footing and my fishing rod.

"Oof," was all I could manage to grunt out as I leaned back into my seat, struggling hard not be pulled overboard by what seemed—to me, at least—to be the granddaddy of all Chinook salmon.

"Tkzzzzzzzzzzzzz!" the reel howled again, as the fish took off downstream, trying to shake the sharp barbed hook from his jaw.

"Yeah, buddy! I think you got yourself dinner!" Trapper shouted over the whine of the line.

"Oooof," was, again, all I could muster as I leaned back against the pull.

If there's anything that any feline likes more than catnip, it's fish. I'm no different. I can't get enough of the scaly, slimy creatures. And my hometown is one of fishing's legendary hot spots.

Fishing on the Beaver Butt River—as well as just offshore from the twin coastal hamlets of CatsCamp and Dogstown—has always been a mainstay for the residents here. Both the commercial and recreational fishing industries have drawn the majority of revenue into this portion of the coast since rape-and-pillage-style mushroom harvesting was outlawed in the last revolution.

While I won't turn my nose at snapper, cod, or eel plucked from the cold ocean waters, my favorite has to be a large salmon steak fresh from the river. Normally, however, I catch my fish down at Fins 'n Fur, a local seafood market run by a dog-and-cat couple. I have always left the hard work of actual angling to the fishermen, but today I agreed to try my paw at it.

Trapper, a stout black lab—and one of my best buddies—talked me into getting up sometime around oh-dark-thirty and meeting him down at the Dogstown Municipal Boat Ramp. He said it "would take my mind off of things." I knew what "things" he was talking about, so I reluctantly agreed.

We put his old wooden boat in the river and slowly motored away from the public dock just as the sun was coming up over Frog Tongue Mountain to the east. It was a beautiful sunrise—the sky aflame in a cavalcade of pinks and oranges, purples, and reds. The mist rising from the water as the night's chill gave way to the warmth of day. We were right along the fog line. To the west—out over the ocean, beyond the breakers blocking the bay's entrance—the sky was an ominous dark bluish-black.

I manned the small six-horsepower outboard while Trapper baited two hooks, slowly and methodically threading and tying a frozen herring onto each one. He tied one of them to the line coming out the reel attached to a sturdy seven-foot-long fishing rod. I wasn't paying much attention. I was barely awake, slightly hungover, and becoming a bit queasy with the smell of the bait, the rocking of the boat, and the fumes from the two-cycle engine.

"Hey! Duke! Wake up! Watch where we're going!" Trapper shouted.

I must have started to nod off, because all of a sudden—from out of nowhere—a large channel marker buoy was less than ten feet from the front—I mean "bow"—of our boat. Big, green, and made of steel, with its bell clanging and green light flashing. I had just enough time to jam the motor into reverse and steer hard to starboard (that's to the right for all you landlubbers) and miss the buoy.

"Wow. Hey…uh…sorry, Trap," I said. "It's the first time I've driven a boat since I was a kitten. And that buoy must be drifting in the current or something. Did you see the way it was just…there?"

"Duke, that buoy hasn't moved in decades, and your chin was on your chest. You were passed out and drooling, I can see the wet spot on your life jacket. Now get with it, this could be dangerous, 'kay? If something happens, and we stall, the outflowing river current will take us right into the jaws of those breakers there." He pointed to the lines of whitewater stacking up on the horizon. "This little boat will be splinters in seconds, and you and I will be just as much bait as this herring here. Our only chance would be for both of us to grab those oars and paddle like crazy toward shore. We'd end up on those rocks inside the jetty. My boat'd be toast, but we'd survive." He paused for a couple of seconds to let that sink into my befuddled brainpan. "Got it?" he asked pointedly, jabbing the point of his finger into my chest.

"Uh…okay. Sorry, Trapper," I apologized. "I'm okay now. Honest."

We putt-putt-putted out into the main stream of the Beaver Butt River, the little outboard burping exhaust. I powered the engine down to a slow troll and steered the boat into the lineup of other fishermen on the water. There were close to a hundred other boats on the water, and with so many in the bay—all of us trolling for the same fish—cooperation was needed between all of us. Everyone trolls at about the same speed and follows one another upriver as far as they think the fish could possibly be, and then they pull in their lines, turn the boat about and troll back downriver until it's time to turn again. Everyone goes up and down the river; going across would mean snarled lines and frayed tempers. As soon as we had taken our place in the circuit, Trapper dropped one line into the water and let it play out until he felt the bait hit the bottom. He then reeled in four cranks of the handle so that the bait wagged behind the boat and just six inches or so above the floor of the river. The larger salmon lay in the coldest water along the bottom, and we wanted our bait to be right in their faces. We had to make it as convenient as possible for some big ol' lunker to take advantage of the tasty snack we were offering. Trapper let out the bait from the other rod's tackle and put both rods into the rod holders mounted on each side of the boat. We settled in to wait, slowly motoring east, upstream into the sunrise. Trapper took over manning the engine, and I sat down facing the stern of the boat, keeping my eyes on the two rods, trying to keep awake.

Ten minutes after we had dropped our lines into the water, I got a strike. I saw the rod on the left—I mean "port"—side bend over in half and instinctively grabbed it out of the holder. It felt as though the rod had come alive and was determined to yank my arms from their sockets. Trapper yelled at me to pull back hard on the line to set the hook into the fish's jaw, but it was all I could do to keep myself from being heaved over the transom and into the river. By the time I recovered from the shock and got my feet underneath me, the fish had spit out the hook.

Trapper laughed. "Well, it's not as easy as it looks, is it?"

We switched positions so he could rebait my line while I drove. "It might seem kinda dull just motoring up and down the bay, but you have to stay alert, pal," he said while threading another herring onto my line. "You have to watch your line, the other lines in our boat, and keep an eye on what's happening in the other boats around us. If they get a fish on, we all have to reel ours in until we're away from the area. If they have a fish on the line and it gets tangled in our lines, and he *loses* his fish, well…it wouldn't be good. I've seen some nasty fights break out over fish lost like that."

By then he had finished baiting my hook and dropping it to the right depth. We traded seats again, and I sat down with my rod in my hands, this time paying much more attention to what was going on, on the river. The sun had come up a bit, and it was much lighter out. The mist had burned away, but the fog had moved in a bit closer, giving the whole scene a spooky Halloween feel to it. There was no wind. Everything was quiet, and you could catch snippets of conversations from other boats around you. Sound travels easily over such still water. Every once in a while, someone would holler that they had a fish on the line, and we'd look around to see if it was one of the surrounding boats, but it never seemed to be near enough to us to warrant stopping what we were doing.

Within a half of an hour, Trapper had hooked a nice twenty-five-pound salmon. I took over manning the engine and tried to keep us slowly following the fish's lead. The other boats around us all reeled in their lines and steered clear of us as Trapper slowly hauled his fish toward our boat. When he could feel the fish beginning to tire, he told me to put the engine in neutral and grab the net. As he got it closer to the side of the boat, I could see large flashes of silver, as the fish thrashed back and forth, trying to get away. Eventually, we worked it into the net, and after making sure that it was a "legal" fish, Trapper gave it three solid whacks on the top of its head with an old piece of sawed-off pool cue that he calls his Pacifier, and we threw the dead fish onto the ice in the cooler in the front of the boat.

For the next two hours, we trolled around the bay, dragging our bait up and down the estuary at the mouth of the river in the parade of other fishermen trying to catch the same fish. Every once in a while, the crew on a boat here or a boat there started jumping and shouting, but on our boat it was pretty quiet until all of a sudden, my reel started to scream.

"Tkzzzzzzzzzzzzzz!" the fishing reel sang as another fifty yards of twenty-pound test screamed off the spool.

"Woooo-hoooo!" Trapper yelled again.

I think he was more excited now than when he caught his. Another boat that had been trolling behind us and off to our side hadn't pulled in their lines and continued on its path past us and came within shouting distance.

"Hey! We've got a fighter here! Pull your lines in," Trapper barked at the two old dogs in the boat. They stared at us, but just kept motoring in our direction.

"Is that you, Trapper?" one of the old dogs yelled. "I recognize the boat, but don't know who your crew is."

"Yeah, Lex, it's me," Trapper growled. "And this is my buddy Duke. And he's got a fish on, so stay clear!"

"Shoot, Trap. He looks like a cat! What's a cat doing on your boat? And tell me why I should worry if your little kitty-friend loses his fish," old Lex shouted, glancing at his fishing buddy with a smirk.

By this time, they were within fifteen yards of our boat, and my fish was not giving any indication that he was ready to be landed. As a matter of fact, right then he took off on another run, pulling an additional twenty yards of line from my reel and heading right for Lex's boat, which was still closing in on our stern starboard quarter.

"Get outta here! Stay back!" Trapper barked. "We've got a big one on!"

My line went slack enough for me to start slowly reeling in, but the fish was still swinging around in the direction of their boat. I reeled in frantically, not wanting my fish to swim under them, pulling hard against the strain. But it was no use, the tight line rubbed against their hull and broke off abruptly, sending me flailing backward, falling painfully hard against the inside of our boat. I stood up with the rod in my hands, line flagging in the slight breeze, rubbing my back where it had slammed into the railing.

"Ha! Well, it looks like you lost that one, kitty," old Lex laughed. They were right next to us now, just ten feet from the side of our boat. "Good thing it broke off, 'cause if it would have fouled our lines, we'd have to kick your furry little cat butt."

"Yeah. You're not hurt, are you?" the other dog asked with mock sincerity. "Why don't you go back to shore and have a saucer of warm milk. That'll make it feel better." The two of them howled with laughter as they slowly motored past us, lines still trolling behind them.

Trapper was seething. He growled to me under his breath, "Hang on, Duke. We're about to have a change in course."

I sat down just as he gunned the engine and cranked hard to the side, swinging the bow of our boat mere inches from the stern of theirs. He cut the engine, and we coasted over the fishing lines trailing from their boat, getting the monofilament hooked on our now still propeller and yanking both of their poles right out of their rod holders and into the river with a pair of splashes.

Trapper stood up and in a stern and quiet voice, said, "Oops. Sorry, boys. It looks like *you* got *your* lines tangled in *my* prop." He pulled the engine up out of the water and freed the nylon line. Trapper stood there with Lex and his buddy's lines in his paw. The two old dogs stood in the stern of their boat, engine shut off, jaws hanging open. "I'll bet you guys would like these back, wouldn't you? Those looked like some expensive reels and maybe even custom-made rods."

Lex was the first to regain his composure. "Okay, Trap. Just give us those lines. We can haul our rods back in and call it even. We've all had our fun, right?" They were drifting closer toward us.

Trapper looked at me and back toward the two old dogs. "No, Lex. We *all* haven't had our fun. Have we, Duke?" He looked over his shoulder at me.

I stood silent, rubbing my aching back.

"You two had some *fun* when Duke lost his fish. I had some *fun* when I watched your rigs hit the water." He let the lines drop from his paw. They disappeared into the brownish-blue water. "And now Duke has had *his* fun seeing the look on your stupid bigoted faces as you watch your favorite tackle sink away. Let's go, Duke, there's fish to be caught."

I dropped the engine back into the water and started her up. We motored slowly away from the two old dogs, who stood there gaping at us incredulously. Some of the other boats in the vicinity gave us the thumbs-up, mainly the cats in the other boats. The other dogs were pretty quiet for the most part. It seemed that most of the fishermen on the water—dog or cat—had had enough of Lex and his rednecked ways for long enough. But some of the others just trolled on by, either genuinely oblivious to the event or silently agreeing with the old dog's old way of thinking.

"I have the feeling we're gonna hear about this little incident when we get back to shore, Duke," Trapper said. "But in the meantime, let's fish. Here, you drive and I'll re-rig your line for ya." He stood up, and we switched places.

Trapper dropped his line back into the water and put his rod into one of the holders while I maneuvered the boat back into the lineup. I glanced around at the other fishermen around. Most of them had shrugged off the incident as merely a distraction to the business at hand—fishing.

But the pair of codgers weren't going to go quietly. They started shouting general obscenities in our direction as we trolled away from them. I couldn't make out the exact words, but the gist of it was that we hadn't seen the last of them, that we didn't realize who we were dealing with, that somehow—someway—they'd get even, and what the heck was this world coming to when a dog stood up for a cat!

"Yeah, Trap," I said as my fishing buddy dropped my line into the river and let it sink to the bottom. "We're both gonna hear about this one. I hope it was worth it."

"Don't worry about it, Duke. For the most part, dogs and cats get along better out here than on land. There's just a couple old cranks like Lex who give all of us canines a bad name."

We trolled up and down the bay for a couple of hours, and each of us caught another fish apiece. Trapper said that the bite was on; cats and dogs all around us were reeling in fish. We totaled out with three nice salmon as we pulled into the dock by the boat ramp. I stayed with the boat while Trapper went to get the trailer. While I was waiting, Ginger Larson, the co-owner and only reporter from the feline weekly paper, the CatsCamp *Distorter*, hurried down the dock, camera hanging around her neck.

"Why, Dukie!" she squealed. "What are you doing down here? I didn't know you were a fisherman. How'd you do out there? Wow! Look at those fish! Is this your boat?"

Before she could utter another question, Trapper backed the trailer down the ramp, and we started to secure his boat to the winch at the front. Getting out of the car, he coolly said, "Hi, Ginger. Slumming for a story on the canine side of the river?"

Apparently there was a little bit of history between the two. Ginger gritted her teeth into a somewhat sinister grin. "Hello, Trapper," she said icily as she put her camera away. "I was just talking with Duke here. I should have known he was here with you." She started walking up the dock toward the parking lot and said over her shoulder as she walked, "Duke, call me this afternoon or on Monday. I've got some really big news for you." She winked as if to imply that it was something just for me and not for Trapper.

Still looking backward, she walked right into Trapper, who was hunched over tying off the anchor line to a cleat on the side of the boat. He stood up quickly and knocked poor Ginger—cameras, cell phone, street clothes, and all—right off the side of the dock and into the shallow water of the boat ramp. The ramp was only knee deep, but covered in a thick bright green carpet of slimy, slippery algae. As she stood up, soaking wet, her shoes slid out from under her, and down she went again, landing on her back in the algae. Trapper roared with laughter as he climbed into his van and pulled the boat and trailer up the ramp. I reached into the water to offer a hand to Ginger, but as she reached for my hand, she slipped again and went down, this time face-first.

I couldn't hold back anymore and just had to start laughing. Trapper, watching the whole thing from his rearview mirror, climbed down from his van and strolled down the boat ramp dock with the smuggest look I've ever seen on anyone's face, carrying a rope and a life preserver. He tossed the end of the rope to Ginger and pulled her to the dock, where he and I dragged the soaking wet feline woman up onto the pier.

We were laughing. She was crying and shivering. I offered her my jacket, but she just waved us off. "Get away! Both of you. Just leave me alone."

So we did. We drove off in Trapper's van toward his home up on the bluff overlooking the ocean. Seeing Ginger in the rearview mirror as we drove away, I just couldn't help feeling sorry for her and wondering what really big news she had for me.

CHAPTER 2

I Tried Smoking Salmon, but I Couldn't Keep It Lit

Up at Trapper's place, he pretended how to show me how to filet a fish, and I pretended to pay attention. He put three salmon sides in a plastic bag for me and threw the other three in the fridge in his garage. We walked out to his driveway, where my 1970 Plymouth Valiant—Prince Valiant, as he's affectionately known—was waiting.

"That was pretty fun today," I said to Trapper as I opened up the trunk and pulled out an old Styrofoam cooler that still had a couple of empty beer cans floating in an inch of yucky water—the remains of a surf session from earlier in the week. I gave Trapper the cans. "Keep the deposits," I said and poured the water off the edge of the driveway before dropping the bag of fillets into the styro-box. I fired Prince up and drove down the hill toward town.

You know, sitting and shivering in a boat all day can really wear a cat like me out. Fishing is a lot like surfing. You wait around in a constant state of readiness for short bursts of excitement. And, I have to be honest, hooking, fighting, and landing a thirty-pound fish is almost as fun as dropping into and riding a head-high glassy wave—not quite, but almost.

I headed over to the Stump and Grind for a little warm-me-up. The Stump calls itself a "feline local's adult beverage establishment," another term for a cat's tavern. While canines are surely welcome—Madge, the owner/bartender/cook, will happily take anyone's money regardless of what rung of the evolutionary ladder their ancestors fell off—most dogs willingly avoid the place. You couldn't really blame them. The building sags a little toward the creek that runs along the side and has its share of septic problems, resulting in a pungent aroma that wafts from the area of the bathrooms every time it either rains or Madge runs the dishwasher.

Once known as "Bad Madge," she's an old manx who was really someone to purr over before the age of electricity. Madge can pour a mean drink, though she rarely remembers what's in it. This has been her bar since her husband died mysteriously after eating snail bait. Her tattoos have long since blurred to look like permanent bruises. Her attitude has also mellowed a bit over the past fifty years of working the backside of the bar.

Seeing as I just got done fighting and filleting a couple large salmon, I smelled like fish, and usually, I love the scaly aroma, but right now it was a little rank. Madge saw me come in and automatically poured me a glass of Drab Light. I nodded toward Tater and Fang, who were holding down their end of the bar, and she poured each one of them a shorty as well.

Tater and Fang are two grumpy old cats that are as much a part of the place as the barstools they're forever perched on. They love to sit there and argue—sometimes the same point—all day and watch batball on the scratchy old television over the bar. Buying them a beer is practically required.

"Well, look at you," Madge said. "The ol' cat and the sea. A regular Hemingway, huh? I never knew you fished, Duke. You must be getting old or bored, or both." She put the glass of pale stale ale in front of me. "You hungry?" she asked with a sly sideways grin as if there was some private joke bouncing around in her septuagenarian brain. "I could fry up some anchovies and troll 'em over to you."

I must have looked like I was something dredged up at low tide. "Madge. I'm surprised. I thought you liked fishermen. This time of the year, this place is usually filled with 'em. And you can smell 'em from the parking lot." I looked around and noticed that it did seem a little quiet for a Saturday afternoon.

I kinda remember Trapper telling me earlier in the day that the fishing had been a little light this year. There were less and less people on the water each week, as if the season had turned inside out. In normal years, the summer fishing runs start out with a few small fish here, a few medium-sized fish there, and gradually but steadily building until, by the end of August, the river is filled with salmon as big as third-graders. Maybe that's why they're called schools of fish—I don't know. Apparently this year started out with all indica-tions that it was going to be a record-breaking year—the first few fish that were caught were large, and there were lots of them. But since then, the numbers and the size had gradually tapered off. A historical inversion, so to speak.

There were all sorts of rumors why the fishing was like that. Some said that the early success had brought in a lot more fishermen than usual so the fish were spooked from biting. Others said it was just the last stragglers from the winter runs and the summer run hadn't yet kicked in. So-called experts said that they (whoever "they" are) were releasing water from the dams upriver, which was cooling off the water, which made the fish less excitable. Some said that the commercial fishermen offshore were catching all the salmon before they could reach the river. A couple of the old dogs believed that the otters were netting them at night, which was totally illegal, not to mention socially unacceptable. As with anything, or maybe more so in the case of fishermen, if you asked ten people, you'd get two dozen theories. Everyone had an opinion. My grandfather once told me, when I was just a kitten sitting on his knee soaking up everything he told me as gospel, "Opinions are like feet: everybody's got at least one, and besides yours, they all stink." I loved ol' Granpapa, but come to think of it, he kinda stunk, too.

"Hey, Madge," I said to her as she waddled back toward the kitchen to attend to someone else's lunch. "If I bring in a salmon fillet, can you cook it for me?" As soon as the words came out of my mouth, I wished I could get them back. What was I thinking? She was notoriously the absolute worst cook in town. Why would I waste a full third of my bounty from the sea (river actually) in this dump? Sometimes my mouth and my brain seem to be competing with each other to see who could make the rest of me look like the bigger idiot. My mouth just scored one over the brain.

"Sorry, Duke. I can't do that. The Board of Health, Welfare, and Rumor Control would close me down. I have to buy my fish from a commercial outfit. I can't even have your fish in my freezer." She leaned forward and said quietly, "Personally, I think the unions bought themselves that regulation with junkets to Hawaii a couple years back. I wish I could. The prices they're charging me these days are more like piracy than anything. Supply and demand, they tell me. And supply has been down this year."

Relieved, I said, "How about a nice piece just for you? I've got more than I have room for, and I'd rather someone ate it than let it go bad. I'll bring you a chunk tomorrow."

"Sure, sweetie," she said, patting my hand. "That's real nice of you—but you're still gonna hafta pay for that beer."

I finished my glass, threw a couple bucks on the bar, said "so long" to Tater and Fang, and walked out the back door to my car. I usually park in the back. I don't want the police watching me as I leave and get behind the wheel. My car is so slow that I couldn't do much damage, but they're always looking for some reason to "talk" to me. Actually, Madge appreciates it when I park back there. She says that when my car's out front, it makes the place look even more run-down than it is. As I was crossing the back lot, squinting into the late afternoon sun, I almost walked right into Butch Larson, editor, publisher, layout artist, typesetter, and almost everything else of the local gossip sheet, the CatsCamp *Distorter*. He's also Ginger's husband.

The *Distorter* came out every Thursday and was filled with just enough local "news" to make the ads look less obtrusive. When I was growing up, it was published on Tuesdays. Then, while I was away at college, it started coming out on Wednesdays. In a couple years or so, it will probably be a Friday paper. The Larsons were cats, after all, no need to hurry too much. The Dogstown *Bark and Mew* was more of an actual newspaper, but—in my opinion—was highly biased with too much of a canine cant to it.

"Hey, Butch. I saw your wife today," I said, sort of fishing to see if he knew about her little dip in the river.

"Yeah. I just talked to her on the phone. She said that your dog friend pushed her off the dock down at the boat ramp."

"No! No, that's not what happened," I quickly started. "She was walking down the dock and she bumped into Trapper, and—"

Before I could finish, Butch put up his hand and smiled. "Duke," he said softly. "I'm sure there's a bit of truth in both sides of the story, but between you and me, she's been needing a good dunking for a while now."

"No. It was an accident. Really. Trapper was just—" I tried to continue.

"Sure, Duke. Whatever. Don't worry about it," he said with a grin, cutting me short again. "I'm just gonna go in and have Madge make me some lunch while my soggy wife soaks in a warm soapy bathtub." He patted my shoulder and walked past me into the Stump.

Butch and Ginger were good folks, a little feline-centric, but very nice and community-minded. The *Distorter* was always there to help promote charities and fundraisers. Butch or Ginger sat on the board of almost every nonprofit group on the cats' side of the river. They ran their business out of a small office downstairs from the apartment they have been living in since they were in high school. As a wedding present—or a curse, depending on what side of the weekly deadline they're on—they were given the newspaper from Ginger's parents. So for the last twenty-seven years, they've been the feline voice of Carver County.

Along with the newspaper came old Mrs. Walker, who ran the office—collecting bills, answering the phone, and writing the classi-fied ads. She retired a few months ago and was replaced by a young gal fresh out of community college with her journalism degree. Her name is Faye, and I'm pretty sure that since the moment she put her paw in CatsCamp, Ginger has been trying to get us together. Faye thinks it's great. Heaven only knows what Ginger has been telling her about me, but even though Faye is nice and all, she's just not my type. Kinda weird. She's a little bookish and overenthusiastic about things that to me seem like normal everyday stuff. The worst part is that Faye just keeps popping up at the oddest times in the strangest places.

For example, a couple weeks ago, I paddled in to shore from a beautiful surfing session, and there was Faye having a picnic on the beach. Now this wouldn't seem out of the ordinary, except that this particular stretch of beach can only be reached by a hike down a steep cliff with the assistance of a rope tied to a tree. Not only is this little strand of sand hard to get to, it's usually very windy. The swirling breezes throw sand everywhere, and when the high tide comes in, the beach all but disappears under the waves. But there she was, sitting on a beach blanket with sandwiches, salad, lemonade, and a funny sort of smile.

"Hi, Dukie!" she said, waving to me as I got out of the water.

"Oh. Hey, Faye," I said. "What are you doing here? How'd you get down here?"

"I'm just having a little picnic. Ginger said this is a really nice lit-tle beach, and she told me how to get here. She didn't tell me about the rope, though. I kinda fell the last few feet to the sand," she said, show-ing me a patch of scraped skin above her elbow. "Wanna join me?"

"Uh. No. I'm a little cold and tired and wet and sandy."

I started to leave when, in a sort of desperate yet bubbly voice, she said, "Oh, c'mon. I've even brought herring-slaw sandwiches and potato bug salad. I heard they're your favorite."

"You've been talking to Ginger too much," I said. "But a cat like me does get hungry surfing for four hours, and ya know what? A herring-slaw sandwich sounds pretty good." Poor Faye was so excited that I just had to sit down and share her lunch with her. "But, Faye," I said. "My name is Duke, not Dukie. Okay? Do you even know what a dukie is?"

We had a nice lunch, after which we loaded the blanket, cooler, and picnic basket onto my surfboard and hiked back up to the road. We said our goodbyes, and I took off out of there as soon as I could— driving Prince Valiant with my foot to the floor, still wearing my wetsuit. Looking in my rearview mirror, I saw Faye standing on the side of the road with her hand to her head, miming a make-believe telephone and mouthing the words "call me" as I sped away.

She's always doing things like that. I like her and her heart's in the right place and I don't mean to be mean, but I just don't want to spend that much time with her. She kinda creeps me out. I'm going to have to talk with Ginger. She's gotta be behind this.

Ever since I got dumped by Cindy, Ginger has made it her new project to make sure I don't spend my life as a bachelor. Cindy was a sweet gal from the Midwest who came out for the summer and worked at one of the local banks. She was the niece of a friend of my mom. We hit it off immediately, or at least I thought we did.

We went hiking, surfing, and just hung out together. It was wonderful, for a couple months at least. I had just solved the Doggie Crunchies murder case and had a bit of spare change, some notoriety, and most importantly, the inklings of an actual productive career. So, being a cat, I had fun. After a while, Cindy thought I should be getting back to work. Our conversations became more and more one-sided and more and more sprinkled with words like *lazy* and *ambitionless.*

"But isn't that all about being a cat?" I asked, getting out of her car in front of my apartment one night about six weeks ago. I don't think that went over too well with her. The slam of her car door was the last thing she didn't say to me.

Oh well, it wouldn't have lasted anyway. She was looking for a cat to settle down with—a big ol' tom she'd feel more secure with. We had a nice romance going for most of the summer, and just as I thought it was beginning to develop into something deeper, she dropped the bomb on me that she was moving back to the middle of the Midwest and saying yes to the cat who proposed to her last spring. Apparently she wanted to see the Left Coast first, meet some new peo-ple, and decide if she really wanted to settle down. Apparently she did, and apparently I was just a lab rat in her little experiment.

Surfing doesn't seem the same these days. She was getting into it, and now, when I paddle out into the waves, it just reminds me of her: her smiling and laughing and splashing in the foam. She wasn't much of a water cat, never going deeper than she could stand and still keep her chin dry, but she sure looked good in a wetsuit. And I miss her.

Being of the feline persuasion, I decided that a nap was just what my fished-out heartsick frame needed. And I knew just the sunbeam to curl up into. It was waiting for me at home, beaming into my living room, landing on my sofa.

Now that we're into autumn, the surfing can be really hit or miss—great every once in a while, but lousy most of the time. The waves have been pretty flat. We're still waiting for that first winter swell. So I've been spending more time than usual vegetating on my little couch in my little apartment feeling sorry for my little self. And the root of my personal pity party? Women, of course.

I wonder if I could have changed enough to entice Cindy to stick around. But I keep tossing that idea away. It took me a little more than three decades to become the cat that I am. Changing into one that would fit her mold would be hard, if not impossible. And then I wouldn't be Duke Hazzard, PI., I'd be somebody else, someone that neither of us might like, and then I'd be doubly miserable.

And then there's Faye. Right. Back to Faye. I doubt if I could ever change enough in that direction to make her seem attractive to me. At least not without a partial lobotomy. She's just crazy, and that's the last thing I need right now, a psychotic girlfriend. It's not that I hate her, I just think she's obnoxious.

I stopped on my drive home at the little Quicki-Mart down the street from my apartment to pick up some beer, a little catnip, and today's *Bark and Mew*. The weekend edition of the Dogstown paper is good for some mindless entertainment, gossip, and crossword puzzles.

The Quicki-Mart was empty except for the owner in his cus-tomary position. As usual, Nasim was standing behind the counter. He was a dark-skinned long-haired ferret who sometimes wore a fez, sometimes a turban, and spoke with a heavy accent from somewhere far away. I never could place where his accent originated, and when-ever I asked where he was from, he'd simply reply, "From the very much east of here."

Whatever. Sure.

"Ah, hello, Mr. Duke. How are you doing today?" he asked, smiling a grin with two full rows of big bright white teeth.

"Good. I even caught a couple fish today, Nasim," I said, taking credit for one of Trapper's catch. "And now it's naptime."

"Mr. Duke, I never knew that you did the fishing. Do you have the boat?" he asked.

I couldn't tell if he was making small talk or genuinely interested, I just wanted to grab a six-pack and keep going home. "Uh, no. I went with a buddy."

"Would you like boat? I have one for sale. For you, my friend, very cheap, too," he said, excitedly, almost laughing. "Of course, you pay cash," he added, suddenly seriously, as he rounded out from behind the counter, after making a point of locking the cash register. Okay, now I got it. All of a sudden, he's my friend. Normally, he's pretty cool toward me, but since the Doggie Crunchies case—plus the fact that I finally paid my long-overdue tab—he's all grins and giggles.

"It is right back here outside Quicki-Mart. Come, come!" Leaving my purchases on the counter, I reluctantly followed Nasim out the back door of the store. I really just wanted to get my stuff and go home to the sunbeam waiting for me on my couch, but the little ferret had my curiosity piqued.

In the shade of a sprawling coastal cypress was, I guessed, a boat on a trailer. Well it might have been a boat half a century ago or more. She was a wooden McKenzie-style driftboat, the kind the pioneers built to battle their way down the treacherous turbulent western rivers. And it looked like that was the last time it had seen a coat of paint or any type of maintenance whatsoever. It was so full of dry rot you could poke your finger right through the side of it. It was held together with plywood patches, rusty screws, speaker wire, and duct tape. The trailer that it sat on was what appeared to be a jumble of rusty metal pipes and tubes with a pair of flat tires. Two flimsy pieces of rope connected the "boat" to the "trailer." Looking closer—but not too close, mind you—it looked like if I was to cut either section of rope, the whole thing would collapse into a pile of rust, dust, and splinters.

"Yeah, Nasim," I said. "Nice. Look, I just want to pay for my beer and newspaper and head home, okay? It's been a long day."

"You don't like boat?" Nasim asked, feigning disappointment and surprise.

"No. Not for me," I said, starting to walk back into the store. "Wait. Mr. Duke. You make offer," he said, following behind me. "I give you good deal."

"No thanks, Nasim," I said as we reached the front counter of the Quicki-Mart. "How much?"

"For you, my friend," he leaned forward and looked first left and then right with those beady little ferret eyes. "Okay. You tell nobody I give you good deal. Five hundred dollars."

"What?" I asked incredulously. "Five hundred dollars? For a six-pack and a newspaper? How much for this?" I pointed to the things on the counter.

"No, Mr. Duke. Five hundred dollars for boat *and* trailer. Five hundred eight dollars and fifty-eight cents if you want this, too." He waved his finger over the beer and the paper.

"Nasim," I said softly. I waved *my* finger over the beer and paper. "This is all I want. Eight fifty eight, right? Here." I counted out eight dollars and sixty cents. "Keep the change. And the boat." I picked up my purchase and headed for the door.

"Mr. Duke!" Nasim called after me. "I give boat to you for four hundred, but no trailer. Okay? Deal?"

I had just stepped out the front door and back into the sunlight. I stopped and turned, squinted a little, grinned a little, rubbed the day-old stubble on my chin a little, and looked up as if I was actually considering his offer. His eyes got wider, and he leaned over the counter, looking at me in the glare of the parking lot. I leaned forward a little bit. The only sounds were the hum of the coolers against the side wall and the sound of Nasim anxiously wringing his hands together in anxious anticipation of what he thought—no, what he knew in his bones—must be a sure sale. I took half a step closer, leaned even further forward and softly whispered, "No. I don't want the boat."

I straightened up, exhaled a deep breath, and walked outside to my car, giggling to myself. "That was fun,' I said softly to myself. You know, screwing around with that guy always cheers me up.

I went home determined to finally fall asleep in the sun on my sofa. My apartment is small, dirty, and sparsely furnished, but the couch is positioned to take the full brunt of the afternoon sun. It's a second-floor studio apartment in a fourplex that was built as housing for the cannery workers who yanked monster salmon from the Beaver Butt River back before color photography. It's the typical bachelor pad, dirty laundry on the floor and an empty jar of pickles in the refrigerator. I put five sixths of the six-pack of brew that I picked up at the Quicki-Mart alongside the pickle jar and in front of the two crusts of moldy bread. I opened the remaining beer and took it and the newspaper to my warm, comfy sunspot sofa. A quarter of the way through the front page and an eighth of the way through the beer, and I was snoring like an out-of-tune outboard motor.

Four hours later, the sun had continued on its trek toward the ocean and was just about to set into the sea. I woke up from my nap and, feeling hungry, instinctively went to the fridge. "What am I going to do for dinner? There's nothing here except five of the six bottles of brew I brought home from the Quicki-Mart," I said aloud to no one.

"Oh shoot! The salmon!" The three fillets had been in that old Styrofoam cooler in the trunk of my car, parked in the sun since early afternoon. I ran out to Prince Valiant, sitting in the lot, still basking in the sun. As soon as I opened the trunk, the stench practi-cally knocked me out. I brought the fillets up to my apartment and threw them in the sink. I ran cold water over them, and they started to smell not quite so bad. I emptied the three ice trays from the little freezer compartment of the fridge into the sink and called Trapper. "What do I do with this stuff? I asked. "Is it just trash now?"

He loves to give me a hard time, and today I didn't disappoint him. After a quick and to-the-point lecture in full Trapper style, he told me to continue rinsing them and rub any bit of slime off them, then bring them over to his place.

"I'm just throwing one of my fillets on the grill. One of the others we seal-a-mealed and put in the freezer. The third is going into brine overnight and then into the smoker tomorrow. We'll smoke yours up, and by tomorrow night we'll have fresh smoked salmon," he said. "We're almost out of beer, so pick up enough for me and Roxy and come over for dinner. Roxy says she's got some hot pickles fresh out of the garden for you."

I fished out my cleanest dirty shirt from the bottom of my closet, slicked down my hair, put the fish and the ice back into the styro-cooler, and jumped back into my car. The old slant-six engine cranked right up, and soon we were headed south on the bridge that crossed the Beaver Butt river. Trapper, being canine, lives with his wife, Roxy, on the bluff overlooking the ocean about two miles south of Dogstown. From his deck, you get an eagle's eye view of one of the most consistent surf breaks on this section of the coast. Roxy made him change their phone to an unlisted number because he was getting so many calls from surfers wanting to know if it was worth paddling out that she could barely use the phone herself. She said either change the number or start charging a dollar a call.

I stopped at McRay's Market in Dogstown and picked up a couple twelve-packs of beer on my way over to Trapper's place, then drove up the steep driveway to their house. The door to the house was open, and I brought the cooler with the fish and one of the twelve-packs into the kitchen, where Trapper was busy preparing a sweet and salty concoction.

"Hey, Duke," the big black lab said. "You're just in time. The brine is cooling, and we're fresh out of beer."

He was wearing his usual surf shorts and sandals and an old T-shirt that was covered in stains of fish blood and barbecue sauce. He's a good cook, but not the neatest dog in the kitchen. Roxy was sitting at the counter doing a Sudoku puzzle and talking on the phone. I opened a trio of beer bottles, handed one to each of them, and took a huge gulp from the third. We took the salmon out of the cooler and sliced it into three-inch chunks. Trapper put the chunks of fish into two large plastic containers and poured brine over them. He dove his arm into one of the containers up to his elbow and stirred it all up completely. I did the same with the other. After washing the fish scales off my hands, I put the lid on the container and followed Trapper out to the garage, where we placed both containers into his "beer fridge."

"That's a lot of fish," he said. "I hope it all fits in my smoker. It should be pretty tasty. Your fish wasn't as bad as I thought it was when you called. We'll let it soak in the brine overnight, and tomorrow morning I'll load up the smoker. By this time tomorrow, you'll have enough smoked salmon to keep you happy for a few weeks."

"Cool. Thanks!" I said. "You take good care of me, Trap."

"Yeah. Everybody has a charity, and you're mine," he said with a hearty slap on my back. I couldn't tell if he was completely joking or not. "Okay, let's fire up the grill and burn some dinner."

We strolled back into the kitchen, where Roxy was just hanging up the phone. "That was little Joey, my nephew," she said. "He's just learning how to talk and, just like his mom—my big sister—has a lot to say."

"Yeah, that woman drives me crazy. I've never heard anyone say so much inane things as Elsa. No wonder she's on her third husband. She's wears 'em out, starting with their ears."

Just when I was going to jump into the conversation—having met Elsa a time or two and couldn't agree with Trapper more—I noticed the look that Roxy was shooting at him and decided to quickly change the subject. "Your garden sure looks nice this time of night, Roxy," I said safely.

It was true, with the sun just beginning to give off its warm orange glow, the flowers outside the kitchen window came alive with color, and the tomatoes still on the vine seemed to radiate a delicious red.

"Thanks, Duke. I just finished canning up some jalapeño pickles for you." She handed me a couple of jars. "Don't open these for a month or so to let the flavors age nicely."

Trapper grabbed one of those long lighters—spark on a stick, he called it—and the three of us went out onto the back deck, where he lit the grill while Roxy and I headed to the garden. They had some catnip plants that were taller than I am.

"Those are looking pretty good," I said. I'd been watching them all summer, and Roxy knew that I wanted to sample their crop.

"Duke, I've told you before, those are experimental plants. Just something that we may grow to supplement our hemp crops. When they're ready, I'll make sure you get to test them. But we're still a month or so away."

Trapper and Roxy are boutique hemp farmers. The stuff grows like weeds in our part of the country, and they cultivate about four dozen different strains, mostly as ornamentals, but also several acres of an imported Thai variety that they hybridized with Russian sun-flowers that reach a height of around twenty feet. These they sell to a jobber in the Midwest, who makes it into exotic (and expensive) sustainable flooring. Trapper was getting quite the reputation in the hemp farming community, traveling all around the globe giving sem-inars and such. It was just a funny coincidence that these seminars somehow happened to be in close proximity to some of the best surf spots in the world.

Roxy and I wandered around the garden for a while. She had it arranged by color, with the reds like rhubarb, tomatoes, and red peppers on the west edge to catch the setting sun, and the greens—zucchini, cucumbers, and broccoli on the east side to take advantage of the cool sunrise sunlight. Whether she did that for aesthetics or efficiency, I don't know, but it made for a very picturesque and neatly colorful place.

Soon the salmon was ready, and Trapper was calling us to supper. We ate as the sky grew dark, finishing as the last afterglow of dusk faded into the horizon of the ocean. It was a very peaceful evening, and conversation reduced itself to smiles and nods.

The phone rang, and Trapper took the call. I helped Roxy clear the table, but she wouldn't let me do much else, so I opened another beer and watched her put everything away. Trapper came back into the kitchen and said that it was his friend Osos on the phone. Apparently there was a big swell coming, and the surf should be picking up by Monday, with Tuesday being the big day before the ocean went flat again.

Roxy rolled her eyes and looked at her husband. "You better get going on that report for the Merry Hempsters," she said. That was her name for the trade association the Trapper was involved in. "I can tell already, you're not going to get much done next week. You'll be surfing and fishing, and I'll have to cover your big black butt."

"Don't worry, sweetie," Trapper said, coming up behind her and putting his arms around her waist. "I'll write most of it tonight, and tomorrow I'll spend all day packing up plants to be shipped on Monday. I've gotta be here to keep an eye on the smoker anyway."

"Well, you better. If I have to hang around answering the phone from people who aren't getting their orders, you'll be sleeping in that van of yours!"

I took this as my cue to be on the road. I faked a big yawn and said, "Well, you guys, thanks for dinner. It was great."

"Here, take the rest of this brew, buddy," Trapper said, pulling the remainder of the twelve-pack out of the fridge.

"No, it's all yours. I've got another half-rack in the car. Gimme a call tomorrow, and I'll help you with the salmon."

"Yeah, I know you. You'll help me eat it. That's about all."

He was right. I had no intention of helping him. I mean, I suppose I should learn how to do that, but if I never learn, that's just one less thing I'm expected to do. I am a feline, after all. The expression is "working like a dog." Nobody ever says "working like a cat."

After solving my last case, I've gotten a bit of publicity. Ginger has been my self-appointed press agent. She thinks that it's a con-structive bit of publicity for CatsCamp, whose reputation, in her opinion, could use a little positive updating. Her publicity—she's run a couple stories on me, on the murder, and on the dangerous situations I put myself in to solve it—has also brought in a few cli-ents, so I have a little extra cash these days instead of being con-tinually bankrupt. It basically means that I'm not borrowing beer money from my mother, but it also means more work. And if Osos is correct, there's supposed to be a swell coming in on Monday, so I decided to go to the office on Sunday and get some work done—very un-cat like, and *very* much unlike me. "Cindy should see me now—working on a Sunday!" I laughed out loud to myself alone in my car.

On the way back 'cross town, I called my secretary, Cathie, on my new cell phone. She made me get one, saying that there were times that she needed to get in touch with me, and now that I was being somewhat successful, I should at least act professional. I don't like it too much. It seems it only works about ten percent of the time. She answered halfway through the first ring, "Hi, Duke.

What's up?" she said quickly. I could hear voices and music in the background.

"Well, I was just driving through town and thought I'd give you a call. You gotta party goin' on over there or somethin'?"

"Oh. No. I was just…watching a movie," she said into the phone. Then, muffled, I heard, "Shhh! It's Duke!"

"Really?" I asked. "What movie?"

"Oh, just something my mom wanted to see. I'm not really paying attention to it. I think it's just some old thing."

"Hmmm. Sounded like a party to me. Maybe I could come over and watch it," I said. "I don't have a TV, and it's still early. And I gotta twelve-pack with me."

"Oh…um…no. That's okay. It's just me and mom, and well, you know, she doesn't like to use her hearing aids, so we had the volume up pretty high. You know. And we're both snuggled in our PJ's. It's just us gals having movie night. You know."

I love Cathie like a sister but wouldn't mind if it turned into something more. I knew she had friends over, and that's cool, I just enjoy giving her a hard time. "You sure?" I asked. "I'm just down the street. I haven't said hi to your mom in a while."

"No! Honest. Really!"

"You sure? I don't mind if you're in your jammies." And I didn't, not at all.

"No, Duke. Please, don't come over."

"Okay. Well, you "two" have fun. I think I'm going to head into the office in the morning for a bit. There's a swell coming in this week, so I wanna get some groundwork done on the Moonpie Mountain case."

"Really? You're gonna work on a Sunday morning?" I couldn't tell if she sounded concerned or unbelieving. "Do you need any help from me?"

"Of course, Cath. I can't function without you. You know that," I said sarcastically.

"Okay. I'll see you there at nine. Bye!" And with that, she hung up. By this time, I was only about half a block from her house.

I dimmed my lights and coasted past. There were five cars parked in the driveway and along the curb. The curtains were drawn, but backlit through the drapes, I could see silhouettes of people standing around and could hear the music crank back up. I reached into the twelve-pack in the back seat, pulled a beer out, opened it, and took a swig.

"Cheers, Cathie. Have fun."

I switched my lights back on and rolled off toward my little apartment.

CHAPTER 3

You Otter Be More Careful

I walked up the stairs to my office at 8:45. The door was unlocked, and in the outer room, Cathie sat at her desk, pulling messages off the answering machine. She looked bright-eyed and alert. She was a beautiful long-haired Persian, and for some odd rea-son, she's stuck with me for a couple years now. I'm a lucky cat. Until I solved the Doggie Crunchies double murder case earlier this year, she hadn't been paid for quite some time. She said that somehow she knew that we'd get even eventually.

"Morning, boss!" she said cheerfully. "There's a message for you from Butch. He said to give him a call. He's got some news for you." She chuckled over her little joke. "Get it?" she asked. "Butch. News. Get it?"

"Yeah. I get it, but I think you think it's funnier than I do," I said, smiling and shaking my head. I don't think I'll ever figure women out, especially her. "When did he call? I saw him yesterday afternoon, and he didn't say anything then."

"It must have been last night or something. Anyway, here's his number." She reached over the desktop and handed me a slip of paper.

I went into the other room, which was my office. The view from there gave me perfect sightlines to the mouth of the river as it met the ocean. To the south of the river mouth was a long rock jetty that produced a handsome peeling wave when the swells were out of the north. It also afforded a view of the estuary, with all the fishermen trolling up and down trying to hook a big ol' salmon. Until yes-ter-day, I thought that was about the most boring thing in the world, but now after having caught a couple myself…well, I just might have to go again. It reminded me of the fish Trapper had put in the brine. I wonder if they were in the smoker by now.

I picked up the phone and dialed the number for Butch. I had asked him a couple days before to search his archives and see if he could find anything about a land dispute that was brewing over a large tract up in the hills above CatsCamp. Apparently there was some hanky-panky a few decades back, and the actual ownership of the property is in question. My clients think they own it, but another claim to the property has surfaced by a developer from further down the coast. The whole mess stinks of money, influence, and power versus the nice old couple who are my clients.

After four or five rings, the phone was answered. "Hello," said a female voice that was vaguely familiar.

"Um, hi. Is this Ginger?" I asked.

"No, she and Butch aren't back from church yet. This is Faye." I knew what "church" they went to. They were down at the Stump and Grind for Marge's Sunday brunch. You could have your choice of three so-so meals and a terrific Bloody Mary for just five bucks. It was by far the best breakfast deal on either side of the river—as long as you wanted to eat in a stinky smoky tavern on a Sunday morning. Butch and Ginger were there religiously.

"Oh, okay. I'll try back later," I said quickly, trying to avoid talking with the voice on the other end.

"Duke? Is that you? Don't hang up!" Faye blurted out. "Butch said you'd be calling. I have a message for you."

"Yeah. It's me," I sighed. I felt like I just got caught doing some-thing I was sure to regret. "Hi, Faye. So what's the message?"

"Butch said to meet him here at the newspaper office at 10:30."

"Okay. Great. Thanks, Faye," I said feeling a huge relief, real-iz-ing this was my out and starting to hang up the phone. "Bye now."

"Duke! Duke! Don't hang—"

Click.

Cathie was in the doorway, leaning against the frame with her arms crossed across her beautiful chest. "You shouldn't be such a jerk to her, Duke. She really is a nice girl, and I think you two could be friends if you'd give her a chance," she said.

"Cathie, she's crazy," I said, standing up from behind my desk. "She…I don't know. I mean, she *is* nice and all, but there's just something about her…you know."

"Yeah. I know. She's smart and friendly and pretty, and you like 'em dumb, bitchy, and mean."

"That's not true. I like you, don't I?"

"Hmmph. Listen, *boss*, there was also a message from your mom. When was the last time you talked to her?"

My mother. How do I describe her? My dad passed away a couple of years ago, and my brother, my only sibling, moved to the other side of the country. That left me as the only one in our immediate family within range of her harangues. She's always been the person in charge in our family, and I'm the only one left for her to boss around. I know she loves me—I'm her son, she has to—but she loves giving me grief even more.

"I ran into her a week or so ago in the store," I told Cathie.

Cathie rolled her eyes and walked into the outer room. She picked up the phone and started dialing. I turned and walked to the window to check the surf and watch the fishermen.

"Good morning, Mrs. Hazzard. This is Cathie," I heard my lovely, conniving secretary say. "Yes, it is a lovely morning, isn't it? Yes, that's right. I know. Well, he's right here, and he wants to talk with you. Hold on."

She walked into my office and said, "Line one—it's for you," then turned and walked out before I could say a word.

"I'm docking your pay for this!" I shouted as I walked toward my desk. I heard the outer door close behind her and heard her footsteps on the stairs heading down toward the street.

I took a big breath, picked up the phone, and quickly said, "Hi, Mom! What are you doing tomorrow night? I've got a surprise for you! How'd you like some fresh smoked salmon? I went fishing yes-terday with Trapper, and we caught three fish." My strategy with her is to talk first and fast—don't let her get a word in until the thread of the conversation is firmly on a different track than she was expecting. "Yeah! Three big salmon. No, Mother, I'm not quitting my job to become a fisherman. No, Mother. Yes, Mother, I'm still a private eye. No, Mother…okay, Mom, Mom. Mom! Listen. Can I come over tomorrow night? No, nothing's wrong. No, I don't need to bor-row any money. Mom. Mom! Okay. I'll see you around six o'clock, okay? Okay? Okay, Mom, see you then. I hung up.

"Sheesh. I wish Cathie was here to hear that. She'd know why I try to limit my contact with her to the minimum of what is required of an adult son with an overbearing mother.

By now it was about a quarter before ten o'clock. I definitely did not want to show up early to the *Distorter* office. I figured that I'd need Butch and Ginger to dilute the onslaught of Faye. Hopefully, Butch and I would get to work in the archive room and Ginger would take Faye off somewhere else. I really didn't care where.

I picked up the phone and gave Trapper a call to see how the smoker was progressing, but just got his answering machine. I left a message telling him that I wanted to take some of the smoked fish to my mother tomorrow and then hung up.

After going through my notes on the Moonpie Mountain case for a while, I shut up the office and headed down to the street where trusty Prince Valiant was waiting for me by the curb. I climbed in, fired him up, and drove down to the boat ramp on the CatsCamp side of the bay.

Hanging out at the ramp, waiting until it was time to go over to meet with Butch, I watched two people land fish in the space of fifteen minutes and remembered how much fun that was yesterday. I walked out on the dock and looked downstream to the ocean end of the Butt. There was a line of whitewater where the fresh water melded with the salt, and there were occasional waves crashing and splashing onto the rocks of the south jetty, but the forecasted swell was not even close yet.

"I'm gonna hafta get me a fishing pole. This could be something to do when the surf is flat and there's no wind. And I don't care what

Nasim says, I don't need a boat. I can either fish from the bank or I'll talk Trapper into taking me out."

It was finally half past ten, so I figured it was safe for me to head over to the *Distorter* office. I pulled in the four-space parking lot just as Butch and Ginger were getting out of their car. Ginger waved, smiled a hello, and hurried inside.

"She's running a little late. She's taking Faye to Harborside to do a little shopping and other 'girly stuff,'" Butch said, explaining why Ginger rushed off so quickly.

We went through the empty office of the newspaper and into the archive room. Faye had done a bunch of research for me, made copies, collated, notated, and flow-charted it all.

"Well, it looks like Faye has gotten all this together like I asked. She's working out really well here," Butch said, surprised. Apparently old Mrs. Walker wouldn't have even considered doing a project like that. "Look. She even left a little note for you, Duke."

I picked up the sheaf of papers, and on the top, on a little pink sticky note in a definitely feminine curly handwriting, was a message saying that if there was ever ANYTHING (she capitalized and underlined the word) that she could do for me, I should ask her ANYTIME (again, underlined and capitalized). I didn't know what to think, much less say. She dotted her *i*'s with little smiley faces (at least they weren't hearts!), and I swear there was a hint of perfume on the paper.

"Well, I guess, we're done for the day, huh?" I asked Butch jok-ingly. "If the swell was up, I'd go surfing, but since it's not, maybe I'll hang around the docks like the seagulls and try and pick up some fish scraps. I went fishing yesterday for the first time, and it's kinda fun."

"I know. I saw you at the Stump, remember? Ginger's still a little embarrassed by the whole experience at the Dogstown ramp,"

Butch said. "I think that's another reason why she and Faye had to leave in such a hurry."

Butch and I talked about fishing for a couple minutes, and then he said, "C'mere. I've got something to show you." We went around the back of the building, and in a small shed was a little fiberglass boat on a trailer. It looked a little dirty from sitting for a couple years. "I know it's not much to look at, but it runs and doesn't leak. I got it as payment from an advertiser who left town owing for some overdue bills."

The boat was about fifteen feet long, a deep-vee hull with a 35-horsepower outboard engine on her. She's mostly white, except for a Jordon Almond pink deck and sporting little pink wings like the cars of the early sixties. There were three seats in her, one facing forward for the driver, the other two facing the stern, with a fishing rod holder and a beverage holder next to each seat. Whoever had this boat outfitted it for one purpose—fishing on the Beaver Butt River. The name painted on the stern was "Myrtle."

"Well, *Myrtle* is a pretty cool ol' boat, Butch. Like something from the old movies when everyone was so…glamorous," I said, standing on one of the wheel fenders, leaning over to see the interior. "Not much to her, but all you need for a fun day on the river."

"Yeah. I launched her once since I got it. It's been here taking up space ever since. Maybe we should take her out sometime. I'm not a great fisherman, but I could show you some of the basics," he said. "Why don't we go right now?" he asked. "I got a couple poles. We can stop at Nasim's, pick up some beer and bait, and we're off."

"That sounds good to me! Now that Faye did all my work… well, heck yeah! Let's go!"

Butch backed his old blue pickup truck to the mouth of the garage. We wheeled it out by hand and hooked it up to his hitch. It was surprisingly light and well-balanced on the trailer. I was pretty sure that my car could pull this thing without too much of a struggle. We pulled the boat out into the sun and drove to the gas station, where we put fresh gas in the tank and filled up the tires with fresh air. We swung by my apartment so I could grab a jacket, a hat, and some cash. We stopped at Nasim's for the fisherman's essentials and drove down to the boat ramp, where we launched the boat off the trailer and into the river. It almost seemed like old *Myrtle* was smiling, being back in the water. After a couple tries, the motor sputtered, coughed, and roared to life. Just twenty minutes earlier, she was languishing in her dusty cobweb-filled shed, but now she was Queen of the Bay.

We trolled around for almost two hours and headed back to shore. We had a couple bites, but didn't land anything. We pulled in our lines and motored slowly toward the ramp. "Well, whattaya think, Duke? Do you want her?"

"Whaddaya mean?" I asked.

"Tell you what, Duke," Butch said as he maneuvered up to the dock and cut the engine. "Why don't you keep ol' *Myrtle* here for a couple days and see if you want her. I haven't used it in a couple years, so I certainly won't miss it for a week or so."

"Really? Cool!" I said. I was so excited that I thought I'd kiss him. "You mean it?"

"Sure. Ginger will be glad to see it out of the garage. You can even keep one of the fishing poles for a couple days."

"Really? Cool!" I'm such a stooge, and he knew it. As of that moment, I thought that it was my boat. "Okay. Just for a day or two, right?"

"Sure, Duke. Whatever," he said. "For as long as you need to decide if you want to buy it or not."

"So how much do you want for it, Butch?" I asked. Maybe he didn't catch any salmon, but Butch knew he now had a sucker on the hook.

"I don't know. I'll have to see what it cost me," he said. "But it won't be too much. A couple, three hundred or so. And since it's just been hanging around, I'm not in a huge rush for the cash—I can work out some sort of payment plan."

I could barely contain myself. I was doing a pretty lousy job of being the cool cat. "Really?" I asked for the third time. "Cool!" I said again for the third time.

Butch chuckled as he tied the boat up at the dock. He unhooked the trailer from his truck, and we drove back to the *Distorter* office, where my car was waiting.

I drove back to the CatsCamp boat ramp in Prince Valiant and hooked the trailer up to my car (luckily the ball on the hitch I have fit the trailer). But instead of backing the rig down the ramp to retrieve the boat, I locked up my car, walked down the dock, fired the little pink craft up, and headed out into the bay.

I was just beaming. I thought my smile was so big it would go all the way around my head. As it was getting to be midafternoon and the tide was going out, there weren't too many other boats around. Most fishermen only fish the bay close to the river mouth during an incoming tide. The salmon would rather ride the tide upstream than fight the current. But I didn't know. I only fished for the first time the day before. Additionally, looking at all the others out there, I was pretty much the only one out solo. Almost everyone else had two or more people on board. Hmmm. I wondered why.

"Well, since I'm out here, I might as well try and catch something," I said out loud to my imaginary crew. I baited a hook as best I could remember how to and dropped it into the water. Almost immediately after I set the pole into the rod holder, it bent over and the reel started singing.

"Woo-hoo! Fish on!" I shouted, followed by, "Oh Shit! Now what?" I hadn't been in this position before and could feel a tinge of panic making an inroad into my confused little mind. I was standing there holding on to the fishing pole while my fish was taking out yard after yard of line. I looked around at the other boats, and most didn't seem to realize the predicament that I was in. A couple of them smiled and gave me the thumbs-up and other encouraging signs, but most of the others just motored away from me, realizing that I was going to pull some rookie mistake and they didn't want to be anywhere near a part of that.

"Okay," I said, trying to calm my nerves. "What would Trapper do? Okay. Think, Duke, think." Then, with a flash of inspiration, I remembered, "The net! Right. Get the net out." I grabbed the net with my free hand, and right then the salmon made another run, almost pulling the rod out of my hand. I threw the net down into the boat and grabbed the rod handle with both hands. The reel screamed again as line streamed out. Suddenly the fish turned, and the line slackened. Surprised, I fell backward against the boat's dashboard and hit the kill switch. The engine shut off, but I didn't notice. I was busy reeling in furiously, remembering what Trapper had said about not letting any slack in the line or the fish will throw the hook.

For the next twenty minutes, I fought that salmon. I swear it must have been at least a fifty pounder—and he took me for quite a ride, pulling me way upriver before he started to tire. The fish was tired, but I was totally exhausted. My arms feel like hot heavy lead. My legs were shaking like an old Singer sewing machine. I reached down and grabbed the net with my right hand, holding the rod with my left. I lowered the net over the side of the boat, and as soon as the fish saw it, it dove again. By this time, I was so tired and my reactions so slowed, that the fish pulled the rod right out of my hand while I was fumbling with the net. I stood up, suddenly relieved of the pull of that fish for what seemed like the first time all day, and watched Butch's rod and reel sink into the dark depths of the Beaver Butt River and out of sight forever.

I sat down in one of the crew's seats drained of any and all energy. It was a few minutes before I realized that the river's current was pushing me closer to the open ocean. The little line of white-wa-ter, which looked so tame from a surfer's vantage point, now appeared more dangerous by the minute from the point of view of a single cat in a small boat with no wetsuit. I tried to start the engine, but it flooded, and the old neglected battery gave up before I could get the motor started. I searched around the boat, and there was no paddle. The only thing close was an old water ski that appeared more deco-rative than useful. I climbed up onto the deck and tried using the old ski as a paddle to get back upstream. After a few minutes, I checked my progress with a seagull I located sitting on the jetty. At best, I was staying in one spot: if I let up for even a second, I contin-ued seaward. I looked out to sea, and the swell that we surfers have been looking forward to was beginning to arrive and was building. I realize that a small boat like the one I was trapped in wouldn't survive—it would get tumbled and broken as it was thrown against the huge rocks and boulders that make up the south jetty. I was get-ting closer by the second. I panicked even more, and looking around inside the boat, I discovered that there weren't even any life jackets! I was in full scaredy-cat terror. I jumped back onto the bow deck and start paddling—if that's what you can call it—with the old water ski. My arms were aching from fighting the fish and were positively burning while I paddled furiously, looking over my shoulder as I approached the intersection of the line of whitewater and the jetty. A plan came to me: maybe if the current pushed me close enough to the rocks, I could jump and try and make it. As if to discourage me, a large wave slammed into the jetty a couple yards away from me, scattering drift-wood like matchsticks and covering me in cold salty spray.

I stopped paddling, sat down on the Jordon Almond pink deck, and resigned myself to my fate. *How ironic*, I thought. *A surfing and windsurfing cat like me—not afraid to brave twenty-foot seas on a slight chip of fiberglass—losing his life in such an undignified and stupid way.* Just then, seemingly out of nowhere, a dark, almost black, boat crested a wave between the two jetties and hurtled into the calm water of the bay just in front of the breakers. It sped right past me. I sat there with the paddle-ski in my hands, incredulous, not believing my eyes. The driver of the boat turned and saw me and shouted something under the deck. The boat slowed and turned quickly before motoring up alongside me. Another person appeared from belowdecks with a coil of rope in his hands. As soon as they got close enough, he threw the rope to me and shouted, "Hold rope!" The driver put the boat in gear, and they started picking up speed upriver and away from the breakers. As the slack was being taken out of the rope, I realized that if I didn't somehow brace myself, I was going to get pulled right off the boat and into the water. I wrapped three or four turns around a cleat that was mounted on the deck just as the rope became taut. "With my luck, it will yank the cleat right off the boat and, now with a hole in the deck, I will surely sink'" I said out loud to nobody. "Davy Jones' Locker, here I come." The rope jerked stiff, but the cleat held firm. With the sudden lurch forward, I was thrown back against, and then over, the windshield and landed hard on my neck, knocked silly, in the cockpit of my little boat.

I stood up, a little dazed, and as my focus slowly returned, I saw the backs of three people in the boat that was towing me back toward the dock. But I realized that they're towing me to the south side of the bay—the Dogstown side. I waved my arms and shouted, pointing to the boat ramp on the CatsCamp side of the river, "Hey! Hey! No! Over there! Hey!"

One of the crew turned around and waved back, smiling.

"No! No! No! Over there!" I hollered at them, pointing with both hands at the other side of the river.

The same crew member turned again, smiled, waved, and then realized that I was trying to say something. He tapped the boat's driver on the shoulder and said something in his ear. The driver turned, looked at me, and slowed his boat down. My little boat's momentum kept us drifting forward and up to the stern of theirs. As I got closer, I could see that all three of the people on the boat were otters.

"Where you go?" asked the driver with a smile. "We take you to marina."

"No. No. I go to…I mean, I want to go to the CatsCamp ramp over there," I said, pointing to the other side of the river. "That's where my car and trailer are."

"Hmm. Okay. We go." The driver said something to the others, and the three of them turned around and faced forward. He put the boat in gear and gunned the throttle. This time I was ready, and when the rope pulled tight with a jerk, I was braced against the seats in the cockpit. In seconds, we were zooming across the river to the north shore. Apparently it's "full speed ahead and damn the feline" with these guys.

I haven't had much interaction with otters, but the little bit of contact I have had has been friendly and cordial. They're a reclusive people and tend to keep themselves. The otters—officially the lut-ri-naes—were here long before felines and canines "discovered" this country. When our ancestors arrived, we thought of them as "naked backward savages" who were in dire need of being civilized. Instead of worshiping one single angry unseen god, they paid homage to such uncultured entities as the sky, the wind, the river, the earth, the fish, etc. The name they had for themselves was Chanq-Ku-Wan, which is also the name that they call steelhead trout—arguably the most noble ocean-going freshwater fish on the planet. In addition to our religion, we proudly brought them such things as disease and pollution. These days the otters that used to live on both shores along the entire length of the Beaver Butt River are now reduced to a small town about twenty miles upriver from the ocean called Moleknuckle. It's a quiet hamlet, practically cut off from the rest of the world on the edge of the Chanqkuwan wilderness.

The otters towed me and my little boat right up to the dock at the CatsCamp boat ramp. I untied the rope from the cleat on the bow of my boat and tossed it back to them.

"Thanks!" I shouted. "I really appreciate it! You guys saved my life!"

But before I could say another word, the captain gunned the engine, and they took off upstream, with one of the crew members reeling in the tow rope that was flailing around behind their stern. After he had retrieved all of it, he looked up at me, smiled, waved, and turned around, joining the others in facing forward as they sped away upriver, away from the setting sun.

I was tremendously relieved to be on shore. I swear that if there weren't other cats around watching the whole thing, I would have dropped to my knees right then and there and kissed the ground. But you know us cats—we may be lazy, but we're proud.

CHAPTER 4

WTF? Where's the Fish?

Monday

Early the next morning, I hooked the *Myrtle* up to my car and headed up Riverbank Road toward Moondance Boatworks. I thought I'd take the boat in and have it looked at before I went to work. I had some files to retrieve from the county clerk's office, but they wouldn't be open until 9:00 sharp. Not 8:59, nor 9:01—the clerk is precise, and she'll let you know it.

The best guy who fixes boats in these parts is named Leo Phieu. He's an old one-eyed, fish-smelling Burmese who has inhaled his share of gasoline, paint, and fiberglass fumes over the years. But everyone says that he's "the man" when it comes to boat repair. Leo has been working the river his whole life. He was one of the last actual mail-cats from before there was a road up to Moleknuckle. Moondance is his shop. It's located eight miles up the north bank of the Butt—the cats' side of the river. It's an old dark structure with twenty-foot ceilings and large barn doors that slide open. A snoozing barn owl was perched on the rafters close to the ceiling. The building more resembles an airplane hangar than a boat shop. Tacked around the walls are pictures and newspaper clippings of Leo with old dignitaries, including an ex-president from the forties. There's one picture of a group of men standing on a rock bar with close to forty large salmon laying at the water's edge. A strapping young Leo Phieu is standing in the middle of the crowd, holding up a fish that reaches from his chin to the ground. Just wandering around looking at the memorabilia on the wall is like taking a journey through the history of the river. But the centerpiece of all this stuff on the walls is a stuffed and mounted salmon. Alive, it must have weighed over eighty pounds. When I asked Leo about that, he waved it off as if it were no big deal.

"We used to catch fish like that every day on this river. The ones they call 'button fish' these days, we'd use as bait if we kept them at all. But we were greedy back then. We'd haul 'em in with nets and take 'em by the truckload to the cannery. Then the fishery collapsed. I guess we caught so many fish that there weren't enough to reproduce. The canneries shut down, and everyone had to find other ways to make money. Some of the guys went up into the woods and became mushroom loggers. Me? I was lucky enough to get a job piloting a mail boat. Yeah, I tell ya, those were the days. It was all whiskey and salmon back then. We'd fish all day and then get liquored up and fight at night. That's how I lost that eye, from some old pirate with a hook for a hand. I asked him how he picks his nose with that thing, and before you know it, the whole place was rolling in the mud and the beer and the broken glass. Lucky for me the doctor was there drinking at the time. He sewed it shut, and I jumped back into the brawl. Never saw that pirate again—or his stupid parrot. Then there was the time…"

Leo was just warming up to tell me all about the raucous days of the salmon industry from sixty years ago and I was settling in for a history lesson when a gal in blue jeans, thick glasses, and a pink T-shirt came bouncing into the shop. Her dark hair was hastily pulled into a ponytail—it was slightly off to one side, and a few strands of hair didn't make it into the rubber band. She had crumbs on her chest from what looked like a burnt piece of toast and the remnants of toothpaste in the corners of her mouth.

"Hi, Dukie…I mean, Duke! Sorry," she said, slightly out of breath. "I thought that was your car out there. Wanna beer?"

"Faye!" I said, startled. "Um. No. Um. It's kind of early for a beer. It's only 8:30." I looked at Leo, and he rolled his eyes—his lone eye, I mean—and shrugged.

"But Ginger said that you like beer," she said. "I do, but—"

"Faye, honey," Leo said gently. "Why don't you run down to Howl-Bean and get Duke and me some coffee. Here's some money." He took twenty dollars out of his wallet and handed it to her along with a set of keys. "Take my truck. Use the change to put some gas in it."

"But, Uncle Leo, I can make coffee. It'll just take a minute." Leo pulled her aside and whispered, "Duke really likes the coffee from Howl-Bean."

"Ohhh," she returned the whisper in a conspiratorial tone. "Got it." She winked at Leo and left him and me alone in the shop.

"You can pick your friends, but you can't choose family," Leo said. "Sorry about that. Faye's a sweetheart, a little strange, but she's got a big heart. Faye's father is my daughter's husband's brother, which makes her my grandniece or something. She's got quite the crush on you, I tell ya." Leo laughed and said, "But we've probably got about an hour before she gets back. So let's take a look at your boat."

Howl-Bean is a trendy coffee shop and bookstore on the far end of Dogstown. I figured that she'd have to drive downriver to CatsCamp, across the bridge, and all the way through the length of town. It would take her fifteen to get there, another fifteen minutes to wait in line, fifteen minutes to get gas, and fifteen minutes to get back here.

Leo and I walked out into the large gravel lot outside the shop's big doors. On the trailer behind Prince Valiant was my boat. Faye was backing the truck out of the lot. She winked at me as she drove away. A cold shudder went down my spine.

"Ah. So. The old *Myrtle*. You're the lucky sumbitch that bought this thing. I'll bet it's spent more time in my shop than on the water. I know this boat real well. See this plug right here?" Leo pointed to a chunk of wood that looked hand-carved and glued into a hole in one of the sides of the boat, right where it met the hull. "I had to make that after old Craig Boyds parked it on a rock." He pointed to an odd piece of stainless steel that protruded from the transom. "And this is a custom trolling motor mount I made for Tom Hardly. Ol' Tom was always having trouble with that little motor, and one day got so fed up, he threw the whole thing right in the water and rowed the boat back to the dock. That old redhead sure had a temper, I tell you what. All of us were laughing at him out there. He was so mad his face was thirteen shades of red. Hmmm…haven't seen much of Tom around these days. Who'd you get this boat from?"

"I haven't bought it yet. I'm considering it, though. It's Butch Larson's. He said that he got it from an advertiser in payment for a bill. Butch has had it in the water once. It had been sitting on the trailer for the past three, four years behind the *Distorter* office," I said. I told Leo about my episode yesterday, embellishing only slightly, just enough so that I look more like an unfortunate—and intelligent— seasoned mariner than a panicked newbie idiot who was facing certain death. In my version, I purposely let the fish go 'cause it was too small. "…so the engine stalled and I couldn't get it going again. Luckily, I got a tow in from some otters before anything dangerous could have happened."

Leo looked at me through his one good eye with a smirk on his face. "Hmmm. There must have been two boats like this one out there yesterday," he said, pulling the motor cover off and sniffing in the car-buretor. "I heard from a friend that there was a small fiber-glass boat—I think he said it was white—that almost drifted out to sea. Hmmm."

"Well, it's possible, I guess," I said. "Anyway, before I buy this thing, I wanted you to check the engine. If I have to put a few hundred into the motor, then that changes the whole deal, right?"

"Right," he said, still looking at me sideways. "Come on over here. Lean closer to the engine. Smell that?"

"Smells like varnish, or is that just the fumes around this place?" I asked.

"Nope. That's old gas. When you mix oil and gasoline and let them sit for a while, the gas breaks down the oil, and it gets real gunky. That gunk can coat everything in the carburetor and make the little parts sticky. So the choke won't work, the jets get clogged and don't let as much air in, and the whole engine runs crappy. Nothing worse than old gas."

I was glad he didn't get too technical with me. I can relate to terms like *gunky* and *crappy*.

"When you guys put gas in here, did you just add it to the old gas that was in the tank?" he asked.

"I don't know. I wasn't paying much attention." I replied. "Hmmm. It sure seems to me that a cat of your maritime experience would have noticed that," he said. "Are you sure there were two boats that got towed in yesterday?"

"Listen, Leo. I only know what I told you. Is this a serious problem? How much does something like this cost to fix?"

"A tune-up and a new tank of gas. Maybe a hundred bucks, maybe seventy-five. Right around there somewhere."

I figured that it was a good deal and that I should have him do it. Add to that the cost of Butch's fishing rod and reel that I lost and it was pretty cheap compared to what might have happened if those otters hadn't shown up right then. "Yeah. Go ahead and do it," I told him.

"Okay. I'll have it done by tomorrow afternoon. You might want to invest in a paddle or two and a couple life jackets. You never know when they might come in handy," he said.

"Yeah. I'll see if Butch has those around somewhere."

"Say, did you hear about the otter they found facedown in the river on Saturday morning? He was upstream from Moleknuckle by about ten river miles. I guess he was found by a couple seals. Don't really care too much for the seals. The otters and I get along okay, but I've never met a seal that I trust. Greasy shifty punks, all of 'em." He spat onto the driveway and rubbed the spittle into the gravel with the heel of his boot. "Seals!"

"Nope, haven't heard a thing."

"Aren't you a detective? You should find out who killed him," Leo said.

"Nope. I mean yes, I am a detective, but that's what the sheriff 's department is for," I said. "I've had enough with murders. Let the sheriff and his boys take care of this one."

Leo spat on the ground again. "And that's what I think of the sheriff."

I left *Myrtle* with Leo and headed downstream into CatsCamp. I crossed over the bridge into Dogstown. As I was just getting onto the bridge, Faye passed me headed in the other direction. Her head snapped around as I went by. I stepped on the accelerator and sped up. She crossed the north side of the bridge, turned around, to follow me. I tried to shake her—taking side roads, running stop signs, and finally ending up at the county offices, where I jumped out of my car and started up the steps to the clerk's office. She drove right up onto the sidewalk, slid across the truck's bench seat, and threw herself out of the vehicle, stumbling up to the stairs where I stood watching the whole spectacle.

"Duke!" she said breathlessly. "I got your coffee. Here." She handed me a paper cup that had a white plastic lid and a brown cardboard jacket.

"Why, Faye! Was that you behind me? I thought it was some criminal trying to run me down or something," I said as I took the coffee from her.

By this time, a couple deputies from the sheriff's office across the street came out to investigate, and a small crowd had gathered. Apparently the screeching tires and the impromptu parking job were interestingly out of the ordinary. I lifted the lid off the paper cup and took a sip of the brown steaming liquid. The coffee was actually quite delicious and still hot. "Mmm. Faye, this is really good. Thank you."

"Um, ma'am, you're going to have to get your truck off the sidewalk or I'm gonna hafta cite you," one of the deputies spoke up. The other one was standing a yard or two behind him, resting one hand on his holstered pistol.

She still had the crumbs on her chest and the bit of toothpaste in the corner of her mouth that she had at Leo's place. And in the morning light, she actually looked…attractive in a slightly demented sort of way. I was just beginning to have a change of attitude toward her when out of the blue, she whipped her head around and, glaring at the deputy, shouted, "Hey! Listen, copper, you just stay out of this. This is between me and Duke, so bug off!"

Startled, all I could say was, "Whoa, Faye, easy. These guys have badges and guns."

Her voice continued to rise, "Well, I am so sorry, Mr. Big Shot Detective! I was just trying to be nice, and now you want these goons to haul me off to jail!"

"No! No. Faye. I didn't say that—"

The first deputy turned to the second and said, "Oh, isn't this sweet? A lover's spat right here on the sidewalk. Listen, you two, just move the truck back onto the street, okay? C'mon, Bob, let's get back to work." He turned and started walking back toward the sheriff 's office.

I called after him, "Hey! We're not lovers. She was bringing me a cup of coffee. That's what friends do!"

Faye looked at me, and a huge smile broke out on her face. "'Friends,' Duke?"

"Yes, Faye. Friends. Hey, thanks for the coffee. And thanks for all that research on Moonpie Mountain. I gotta get inside. The clerk's waiting for me. I'll see ya around." I ran up the stairs and into the county office building.

"Yeah…see you around," she said like she was in a daze as I left. Faye was positively floating on air as she walked around the front of the truck and climbed in the driver's side. She backed off the sidewalk and rolled slowly away, taking a right at the light and heading toward the bridge and the CatsCamp side of the river.

I watched the whole process from the safety of the window of the clerk's office. That girl is twisted some way strange, man. I was glad she had that little outburst right then. I was starting to soften up toward her. It brought me back to reality. As it is, I think she might have gotten the wrong message, and this is going to take some fixing. What is it with me and women? One of these days, I'm going to find a nice, pretty, sane girlfriend. I hope.

I was in and out of the office of the county clerk in about half an hour with five photocopied pieces of paper that cost me almost forty dollars. But they held the key to the Moonpie Mountain case—I hoped. The articles that Faye had dug up for me at the *Distorter* held a ton of useless information, but a couple of gems in all that. Now I just had to arrange it all with a timeline, identify the major players and who was lying and who was telling the truth. My hunch was that my clients were right, but I still had a bit of work to do.

On the way back to my office, I decided to swing into Cary's Tackle Box—the local fishing and hunting store and sushi takeout—to see how much a couple of fishing rods and reels were going to cost me. I hadn't even agreed to buy the *Myrtle* from Butch, and already it was costing me plenty. Cary, the owner, a nice old dog who knew everybody and every little bit of gossip in town, welcomed me as I walked in.

"Duke! How's it going? What are you up to today? I heard you bought the old *Myrtle* from Butch. She's a great boat. A lot of fish have been hauled in to that thing."

"Cary, how'd you hear about that so soon?"

"I saw you towing it past my house yesterday, so I called Butch, and he said she was yours now."

"Well, I haven't decided yet. I'm still deciding if I want her or not. I need to price some stuff and see if I can afford to be a boat owner." I pulled out my notebook and started writing down prices of rods, reels, fishing line, hooks, weights, and all the other essentials I'd need to outfit *Myrtle*—and to replace Butch's lost gear.

Cary looked bored and soon realized that he wasn't getting a sale from me this morning. "No problem, Duke. If you need any help, just holler." He walked back over to the gun rack, where a couple of guys were enthusiastically looking at rifles. They had about half a dozen various firearms out on the counter, and each had one in their hands. Both of them were rather short, but looked very muscu-lar, with broad shoulders and thick short necks. Long dark hair that almost looked wet fell out of their backward baseball caps. One of the guys brought a rifle to his shoulder and was sighting down the barrel, and as I stood there watching, he turned and looked through the sights directly right at me.

"Click," he said.

His buddy followed his line of sight and started laughing. They turned their backs to me again and continued talking with Cary.

Cary, being a head taller than the two, looked at me and rolled his eyes in a silent gesture of apology.

I just stood there paralyzed with shock. That was a little creepy. The two were obviously of seal origin. There aren't a lot of seals in our part of the country. The majority of the seal population lives further north. Their lifestyle revolves solely around fish. Their anc-es-tors were here not much after the otters, centuries before canines and felines arrived. They feuded with the otters, but even though they were physically tougher, they were overwhelmed by sheer num-bers and retreated to live among the icebergs and ten-month winters closer to the Arctic Circle. Now, legally, they had just as much right to be there as I did, but right there in Cary's Tackle Box, they seemed as out of place as a miniskirt in a mosque.

Among the bins of brightly colored lures, I found a very use-ful tool—a combination knife, corkscrew, bottle opener, nail clippers, eyeglass cleaner, and flashlight. Whenever you use the bottle opener, a voice comes out of it and shouts, "Woo-Hoo! Fish on!" I just had to get one of those as a gift for Trapper, and took it up to the cash register. The two seals were approaching the checkout counter at the same as I was. They each had a rifle, and one of them had a handgun as well. They also had several boxes of ammunition.

"Go ahead," I said courteously. The two didn't even acknowl-edge me, much less politely thank me for letting them butt in ahead of me. "Is it hunting season, Cary?" I asked the tall dog behind the register.

"Not here, not yet, Duke," he said sternly, trying to make a point with the seals who were oblivious to his intonation. "Up north, though, the season starts earlier and lasts longer. Right, guys?" he added that last part for the seals.

"Uh. Yes, Monsieur Cary. We can hunt almost all year." The first one chuckled.

The other laughed with him and added, "Oui, all the year. Ha-ha-ha." They both had deep low voices and smelled strongly of a combination of fish and garlic mixed with an almost overpowering human odor. These two were obviously strangers to basic hygiene and apparently were boycotting soap, deodorant, and toothpaste.

They paid for their purchases with wet hundred-dollar bills, pulling them out of a roll of bills held together with a leather strap knotted in some ingenious way. Cary put the boxes of shells and bullets into a bag, the larger of the two stuffed the handgun into his belt and the two sauntered out of the store. I went to the window and watched as they headed down the sidewalk toward the Dogstown boat ramp. With their rifles over their shoulders, they looked like something from a bad old Western movie.

"Hey. Sorry, Duke," Cary said as he scanned my multipurpose tool. "The way business is these days, I don't turn anyone away."

"So I thought you couldn't just walk in off the street and buy a gun. Isn't there some sort of 'cooling off' period?" I asked Cary.

"Yep. They filled out all the paperwork ten days ago. Everything's all legal and up-and-up," he said. "I wonder what Ursalik is gonna think about them walking around with those guns, though. They don't have a car. They just walked here from their boat."

Captain Vernon Ursalik was the chief of police in Dogstown, and since they share municipal services, he's police chief for CatsCamp as well. He's an ornery old grizzly bear who has put thirty-five years in on the force and is looking forward to nothing more than the day he retires. He's getting more cantankerous by the minute, believing that anyone who even minutely strays from the straight and legal path is conspiring to delay his retirement. I'm sure he'd blow a couple gaskets if he caught those seals walking through town armed to the teeth.

"So business is *that* bad?" I asked.

"Well, look around, Duke," Cary said, motioning around the store. "It's just you and me. I let my staff off for the day, and if it wouldn't be for those two, I probably wouldn't make more than a couple dollars all day. I mean, look at you. You just come in here and write down prices, buy this little toy, and leave. That'll be ten ninety-five, by the way."

I took out my wallet and handed him my debit card.

"So you're probably going to take your notebook full of prices and descriptions and see how much you can save by shopping on the

Whirled Wide Web, so I lose business to some guy in Omaha. And I lose another four percent for this," he said, holding up my card.

"Oh. Sorry. Here give me that back. I'll pay in cash," I said, pulling my wallet out again.

"No. It's okay, Duke, it's just that this business is so dependent on the whims of nature that it makes me crazy sometimes."

"I thought we were having a good fishing season, Cary. I've been seeing a lot of boats on the water."

Cary walked around the counter and said, "There's a lot of boats, but not a lot of fish. So guys will come over here and fish for a day or two and go home and tell their buddies that it's not worth it. If they were catching fish, they'd stay a couple extra days, buy more bait and gear, and then go home and tell their friends how good it was, and then their pals would come over as well."

"So what's up with the fish, Cary? You sure seem to know more about what goes on around that river than anyone," I asked.

"Who knows? There's just not a lot of fish coming in. The season started out good, but it's dropped off real fast. I've been here all my life and have never seen that before. The commercial guys offshore are doing okay, but they keep saying that there's more boats here than ever before—lots of 'em from…um…up north," he said cautiously.

"You mean like those two that just left?"

Cary just pursed his lips and nodded silently. He obviously didn't want to say anything else on the seal subject. I got a strange feeling about that. "Here's your change, Duke. When you get *Myrtle* back from Leo, bring her around and we'll get her all set for you."

I drove off to the north and toward my office on the other side of the Butt feeling that there may be more to this than anyone was letting on, and probably way more than a lazy cat like myself wanted to get in the middle of.

CHAPTER 5

There's a New Dog in Town

Tuesday morning

I slept in a little on Tuesday morning. I had worked late on Monday, and I was pretty certain I had the Moonpie puzzle fig-ured out. It was going to take one more trip to the county clerk's office. If my hunch was correct, my clients held the claim to the land on Moonpie Mountain, and I'd get a nice big paycheck. If I was wrong, I would still get reimbursed for my expenses. I wondered if Butch's fishing pole that fell to the bottom of the bay could find its way onto my expense report.

After my usual breakfast, which consisted of me listening to my stomach growl while staring at my empty fridge and then heading out to the doughnut shop for a greasy pastry and a cup of cardboard coffee, I headed across the bridge and back to the clerk's offices. The county offices and the Dogstown City offices comprise the majority of a whole city block on the canine side of the Butt. This morn-ing, there must have been some important meeting or hearing going on—there wasn't a parking spot to be had within a quarter mile, so I parked in the alley behind Spanky's Diner. It's a safe spot, and as long as I get a cup of coffee or something, Spanky allows Prince Valiant to hang out there until the lunch crush comes in. I got my second coffee

50

of the morning—that should make me a little skittish—and headed toward the county office building. I took my usual shortcut through Dogstown City Hall. I decided to swing past the ex-mayor's office—now the city manager's office—and give a cheerful "good morning" to Marylou, the ex-mayor's—now the city manager's—secretary. Once the former mayor—Klaus Schickengruber—was sent to prison for homicide and other assorted felonies, the city council stripped the mayor's office of any actual authority that wasn't purely ceremonial. They then passed a resolution and hired a city manager with all the power that the mayor used to have.

I've been friends with Marylou for a few years now, ever since she helped me through the paperwork to get my private investigator's license. She's an older canine who definitely has some pug in her lineage, not too tall, not too pretty—she's actually kind of gross—but she's got a huge heart, and in her position with the city, she's a good person to keep on your side. I rounded the corner, thinking about what information I need to wrap up my case, thinking about the whole Faye/Ginger drama dynamic, and thinking about fishing.

I was definitely not thinking about where I was walking. I turned the corner toward MaryLou's desk and ran smack-dab into CatsCamp Mayor D'Amato—spilling my fresh hot coffee all down my nice almost clean shirt.

"Duke!" the mayor said. "I'm so sorry! I guess I need to watch where I'm going. I'm late for a press conference that Ursalik convened without letting me know. He just called Marylou asking where I was, so I guess I was in too much of a hurry." Mayor Del D'Amato is not only the mayor of CatsCamp but also the father of a beautiful Siamese that I cleared of charges of a double murder a few months ago. He'd always been friendly to me—as any good politician is friendly to his voting constituency—but now that I had saved his daughter from the firing squad and his career from the dumpster, he's been overly nice. I mean, I spilled my hot coffee on myself, and he declared it his fault. "You get that shirt to the cleaners, son. And you send me the bill!" he said over his shoulder as he hurried off toward the county auditorium.

Marylou came out from behind her counter with half a roll of paper towels and handed them to me. "Here, Duke, sop as much of it up as you can. Hurry. Are you okay?"

"I'm fine, Marylou. Thanks."

"Aren't you going to the sheriff's press conference? Didn't you get my message? It started a few minutes ago. What are you doing here? You should be over at the county building."

"Oh…yeah, of course I got your message, and well…I was running a little late, and by the time I got over here, I couldn't find a place to park, so I was cutting through and thought I'd make a quick sidetrack and say hi to you on my way. You know I can't even think of entering this building without seeing you!" I leaned forward and gave her a little peck on her forehead. She blushed and took the handful of wet paper and the now-empty paper coffee cup from me.

"Oh, that's sweet. But you better get a move on, sugar. It'll be over before you get there."

"Right. Well, it was great seeing you. I'd be lost without you, Marylou. Thanks." I turned and hurried off in the same direction that the mayor went. I hadn't gotten more than ten feet when my cell phone rang. Fumbling in my pocket for it and flipping it open—and inadvertently taking a photo of the back of my thumb in the process, I'm still not used to this thing—I answered. It was Cathie.

"Duke, I just got to the office, and there were two messages. The first was from your mother. Apparently you stood her up. Something about a smoked salmon dinner?"

"Oh, shit. I *knew* there was something I was supposed to do last night besides laundry, which I didn't do anyway. Okay. I'll call her later this morning. What's the other message?"

"Does your mother have your cell phone number? Why doesn't she call you at home?"

"I think it's because she'd rather talk with you than me. I'll call her today, okay? What was the second message?"

"The second was from Marylou. She said that there was a press conference at the county auditorium about the otter they found floating in the river a couple days ago. I guess the coroner determined it was a murder—not just an accident. And this time the otters want it publicized. They are pestering Ursalik to treat this as if it was a dog or cat that got killed."

"Right. I'm on my way there. I just ran into D'Amato and talked with Maylou." That was the truth, and all she needed to know about it.

I walked into the auditorium. Ursalik was standing behind the podium, talking with the CatsCamp mayor. The press conference hadn't started yet. I found a seat in the back of the room with the other cats. Normally at these types of meetings, the dogs take the front couple of rows and get there plenty early. We cats saunter in right on time and take the first available seat closest to the door. No sense in wasting any extra energy, right? People think that cats are lazy. I like to think of us as efficient. Sitting in the chair next to me was Ginger.

"Duke! What a nice surprise," she whispered loudly. "What happened to your shirt? So Faye told me yesterday that you two are almost dating."

"What? Dating!" I said a bit too loudly. The dogs up front turned to see what the commotion toward the back of the room was. The Dogstown manager had just arrived. She'd only been in office for a few months—after her predecessor went to prison on a murder charge, thanks to me solving that Doggie Crunchies double murder earlier this summer. The new manager's name is Judy Boodles. She was the mayor of a small town east of here. She doesn't seem to be the mayoral type. She's a small quiet woman in her late thirties or early forties. She looks to be of possible muskrat descent—dark-skinned, thick dark kinky hair, small eyes, thin lips, and kind of stocky. Muskrats are tough people to figure out. They keep to themselves for the most part, have small families, and each one that I've met preferred his or her company over mine. They are very careful and choose each word they say with a good reason. Muskrats highly value their personal privacy—not the usual politician "Vote for *me!*" attitude, for sure.

Right now, there is no mayor of Dogstown. The city council is just waiting for the next election cycle, but as far as I know, nobody wants the job. The mayor is just a little more than a figurehead position. It's really a pretty shitty situation. The office has little authority but all the publicity. So the mayor gets blamed for everything that goes wrong, but has no power to do anything about it. The ex-mayor tried to overstep the bounds of his office and got his tail jerked into a knot.

Ursalik turned to the collected group of reporters and loudly cleared his voice. The canines swung around and perked their ears forward. The old bear looked over them, straight at us, and growled, "If we can get started…"

As the grizzled old grizzly began his speech, I shrank down in my chair, lowered my voice back to a whisper, and said to Ginger, "I told her we were friends. Just friends. Just like you and I are friends. Okay?"

"Like *boyfriend* and *girlfriend?*" she whispered back, smiling slyly out of the corner of her mouth.

"No! We're not *boyfriend* and *girlfriend!* She's crazy!" I said, my voice rising. "She's certifiably nuts!"

"She really likes you, Duke," Ginger said, her whisper getting louder as well. "And she's not crazy. She's just young and…"

Suddenly the room went quiet, the front row canines turned around again, frowning at Ginger and me. Ursalik cleared his throat again and firmly said, "If there's more information that anyone has, they can present it when we're through." He paused and stared at the two of us for a moment for emphasis. "As I was saying," he con-tin-ued, "we don't have any suspects in custody at this time, but there are a few persons of interest that we are keeping an eye on. As soon as we have any information, we will be sure to let you know. Now if there are no more questions…"

Ginger raised her hand and asked, "Captain Ursalik, how do you know this wasn't an accident?"

The dogs up front groaned.

"Okay, Ginger, I will repeat this just for you since your con-ver-sation was apparently too important for you to hear me the first time," he said, trying to reprimand her. "The coroner discovered that there was no water in his lungs, so he didn't drown, and there was a head trauma on the back of his skull. If he fell backwards in his boat with enough force to kill him—which is doubtful—then he would have had to then roll up and over the side of his boat after he had stopped breathing—which is even more doubtful. Okay?"

"Okay, thanks. Just one more question," Ginger said. "Are you handling this investigation? Isn't it on the otter nation and under their jurisdiction?"

"Ginger, maybe we should have a separate press conference just for you and your friend there." He looked at me with those hot red eyes that appear to glow like campfire embers when he's upset. And an upset grizzly bear is like a runaway backhoe: it's best to just get out of its way until it runs either out of gas or over a cliff. "We call these press conferences so that everyone gets the same information from an official source at one time. So I'll repeat this one last time. The Chanqkuwan tribal police have asked us to help with their inves-tigation. Therefore, this will be a joint project between them, the Carver County Sheriff's Office, and the Natural Forest Circus. Okay, Ginger? That's it for questions. If you need more information, you can read it in the Dogstown papers," adding that little dig at the end, prompting a few chuckles and smirks from the front-row boys.

Ursalik rumbled off the stage with the mayor and manager in tow. I stood up to leave, and as I exited, a large sheriff's deputy grabbed my arm and curtly said, "Ursalik wants to see you." He led me down the hall toward the captain's office. I had been spending a lot of time in the county offices lately, and I didn't recognize this guy. He was tall—the top of my head didn't reach to the bottom of his chin—and he was built like Hercules. I tried to shake my arm free, but his iron grip tightened firmly on my bicep. By the time we got to Ursalik's office, the old bear was sitting behind his desk.

"Come in, Hazzard. I'm glad you could take the time to meet with me." He didn't look up while he spoke, just continued reading the papers on his desk. "Ya know, Duke, I don't think I ever thanked you for your help with the Schickengruber case." He looked at me and chuckled. "What happened to your shirt?"

I didn't know what to say. He's never said anything even remotely that nice to me before. "Well, thanks, Sarge," I replied. He hates that. Ursalik is captain of the combined Dogstown and

CatsCamp police force as well as the de facto sheriff of the Carver County Sheriff's Office. The county commissioners have been trying to find a real sheriff for a number of years, but there have been no takers outside of the obvious schemers, scammers, and dreamers. Ursalik has ada-mantly stated on numerous occasions that he is the police captain. Being called Sarge raises the hackles on the back of his twenty-eight-inch neck, something that I love to do.

"Oh, this?" I asked, looking down on the coffee stain that covered as much of my chest as the oceans cover the planet—in other words, most of it. "I…uh…ran into Mayor D'Amato this morning, and we shared a cup o' joe." I looked around for a seat. The captain was being gracious, so I thought I'd make myself comfortable, but the only chair in the place was groaning under the old bear's weight. In the corner, the deputy who "escorted" me in was standing smirking in the corner with his arms crossed.

"So am I in trouble or something? Your stooge here," I gestured toward the deputy standing in the corner, "made it quite clear that I had no choice but to accept your gracious invitation."

"You're not in trouble—yet," Ursalik said, his humor having evaporated. "Look, I got another stiff on my hands, and this whole thing stinks like yesterday's fish. I just want to let you know that we—the *proper* authorities—are on top of this homicide. I wanted to make sure that you know that we'll be much more efficient without your help. Understand?"

"I think I understand," I said, scratching my chin and doing my best to look thoughtful. "Let me see if I got this right: you and your badge-happy boys are going to pretend to find some clues then haul in some obvious guy who will conveniently confess to the crime, and the county will be spared the bad public black eye of three murders in the same year. Am I close?"

"Hazzard, this is a warning. Keep your big feline nose out of this. We'll handle it. Okay? Can you just do that?"

"Listen, Sarge," I said, putting both hands on his desk and leaning forward. "I've got plenty to keep me busy with civil cases. I have no desire to get involved in a homicide."

"Well, that's good," Ursalik said, leaning forward to meet my gaze. "What were you doing at the press conference then? I know you, cat, and I don't trust you."

"Well, I was just walking past the auditorium, and I saw all the cops, so I figured someone was handing out free doughnuts. I thought I'd check it out." That effectively ended the civil part of our little meeting. Ursalik stood up so fast his chair flew away from him and crashed into the wall behind him.

"Get him out of here!" he shouted at the deputy who had been standing stoically in the corner. Hercules took two strides forward and grabbed my upper arm again in his iron grip.

"Ow! Lemme go. I'm leaving," I said, trying to shake my arm from his grasp. Even though he looked like he was predominantly Rottweiler with those huge shoulders and big muscles, it was like wrestling with a boa constrictor: the more I struggled, the tighter his grip became. Pinned to his uniform, which was just a half a size too tight, was his badge, the microphone for his two-way radio, and his name tag. It read "Deputy Joe Wilson." He pulled me out into the hallway and threw me away like I had cooties or something.

Reactively, I started back toward him but stopped short—one of the more intelligent things I've ever done. I looked him up and down while he peered down his nose at me, his lips white with self-re-straint. I knew he could—and wanted to—kick my lazy feline butt, but he knew that I wasn't worth losing his job over.

"So, Joe Wilson," I said. "Hmmph. Yeah, that's a real name. I used that name at the No-Tell Motel just last night…with your little sister!" Why those things come out of my mouth, I wish I knew. Why I didn't just walk away is something I wish I could talk to my ancestors about, them and their gol-durned smart-aleck genes.

In a hummingbird heartbeat, Deputy Wilson had me pinned against the wall on the other side of the hall. "I've heard about you, kitty," he said in a menacing whisper with his face about a quarter of an inch from mine. "And what I've heard ain't good." He put one hand on my face—with the size of his hands, there wasn't room for anything else—and smacked my head into the wall behind me, and then backed away from me. I knew I'd have a painful knot the size of a golf ball on the back of my skull within minutes. My ears were ringing, and there were little black spots exploding in front of my eyes. I blinked a few times—a few dozen times—trying to clear the fog that had suddenly moved into my head, and as my focus returned, I saw the big uniformed official gesture toward me. He did the "two fingers towards his eyes and one finger toward me" move that said, "I'm watching you" that had been so cool a decade ago. The ringing between my ears started to die down, and I heard Ursalik through the open door to his office slam his phone down into its cradle and shout, "Wilson! Get in here. And leave that damned cat alone!"

Deputy Joe Wilson backed away from me and did that two-fingers-one-finger thing again. Before turning into Ursalik's office, he silently mouthed, "I'm watching you, kitty."

I stared at him, returned the two-fingers-one-finger salute, and muttered, "Backatcha, puppy," as he turned away. The difference was I used a different finger—my longest one and pointed it toward the ceiling, not at him.

Rubbing the swelling lump on the back of my skull, I walked into the county clerk's office. Bridgette Maypox, a nice little tabby who is unfortunately for me, very happily married with four kittens of her own, gasped when I walked in. I'm sure I was quite the sight with my aching head, coffee-stained shirt, and those blinking glazed eyes that accompany a concussion.

"Oh my god, look at you," she said, coming around the tall counter. "Here. Sit down. Are you okay? What happened to your shirt?" By this time, I was starting to wonder if people cared more about my shirt than me. "I'm fine," I replied. "But I could use…do you have any aspirin? I'm developing a heckuva headache—this time from the outside in." I showed her the bump on my head.

She frowned, shook her head, and went back to her desk to dig through her purse. We were the only two in the office. "What is it with you men? Between my husband, my three boys, and you, I'm amazed that any male lives past adolescence."

"Well, that's the thing, Bridge," I joked, putting as light a spin on the situation as I could, considering my current state. "We never get out of adolescence." She handed me a couple chalky bitter white pills and a little cup of water, one of those silly pointy paper cones that you can't put down until you drain everything from it or you spill the remainder of the contents. She leaned back on the counter and just looked at me with her arms crossed, frowning and shaking her head. With that look, I'm sure her husband stays in line and her three sons are going to grow up just fine.

After a couple minutes, while I continued to blink hard and rub the back of my noggin, she said, "Well, what else can I do for you? If you just wanted aspirin and sympathy, you would have gone to the County Health Department two doors down. What are you looking for today?"

I told her my theory, and together we began searching through the marriage records from five and six decades ago. As we dug through the files, I told her how I spilled my coffee and about the new deputy. Between her position as underling county clerk and the fact that her husband works for the sheriff 's office, Bridgette has her finger on the pulse of what goes on the county offices. "So what do you know about this Joe Wilson fella?" I asked.

"Not too much. He's only been here a couple of weeks, maybe less. He was transferred from Crows County about two weeks after Boodles became city manager. Rumor has it that he was brought on primarily to be her personal bodyguard—kind of a watchdog. I do know that Bob—my husband—was transferred from his usual forest and river patrol down to the south end of the county and is now on border patrol."

"What? Is there some sort of problem with people crossing the state line?" I asked. "I didn't know it was illegal."

"Bob thinks that Ursalik is mad at him for some reason and just wants him out from under his feet," Bridgette said. "The two never really saw eye to eye. Bob was always too nice and would let too many people off with a warning. Ursalik says his department needs the ticket revenue. Bob thinks that the sheriff 's office job is to help and protect, not hinder and punish."

"So Wilson was brought in as his replacement?"

"Yep. Bob's been with the department for too long to fire, so they just transferred him to an outlying jurisdiction—away from home and family for a week or two at a time—hoping that he'd quit," she said. "We've put in for a transfer back to this part of the county, but we'll see."

"Aha! Found it!" I said. "Here's exactly what I was looking for!" I pulled a dusty folder out of an archive box. "Can you make me two copies of each of these?"

"Sure, Duke. I don't know why you need a marriage license from eighty years ago, but whatever you want." She took the sheets of paper and walked into the back room toward the copy machine. I got up and went around the counter. She came up to the counter, I paid for the copies, she stamped them with her official clerk's stamp and slid them over the counter toward me.

"Thanks, Bridgette. If you find out anything else about Deputy Watchdog, let me know."

By this time, it was the start of the lunch hour. I walked into Spanky's and sat down at the counter. I ordered a burger, fries, and shake. I looked around the room. It was filling up with the usual nine-to-fivers, except for a booth in the corner that was filled with four short, stout, dark-skinned men in sweatshirts and wool caps. They were laughing and talking loudly in broken English, the other language I couldn't discern. As I turned to look at them, they went silent and returned my stare. One of them said something in a low deep voice, and they all turned, laughing loudly. I don't know what they said, but I could tell I was the butt of their joke.

The waitress brought my lunch over to me, and I stood and said, "Oh. Hey. Can I get this wrapped to go? I just remembered something I gotta take care of."

The seals in the booth must have told themselves another joke—at my expense. Their laughter filled the entire diner. The rest of the room was quiet. People were looking around, wondering what was so funny. And since I was standing and they were laughing and pointing at me, I couldn't get out of there fast enough. The waitress dumped my burger and fries in a Styrofoam box and my shake in a Styrofoam cup. I threw a ten on the lunch counter and said, "Keep it. Thanks." I ducked out the side door as quick as I could.

I drove out of Dogstown with a bad feeling about those seals. They seemed to know who I was, but I didn't know anything about them. As a matter of fact, that Deputy Wilson seemed to know more about me than vice versa, too. My sick sixth sense was starting to murmur. It wasn't telling me anything yet, just making a little noise.

Back at my office, Cathie and I spent the afternoon compiling a nice, and if I say so myself, professional-looking, report on the Moonpie Mountain case with decades-old reports from the clerk's office, copies of yellowed clippings from the newspaper that were just as aged, and a summary by Matthew "Duke" Hazzard, PI. That's me—the professional curious cat. We made another copy of the whole thing, sealed it in an envelope, and mailed it to ourselves— just in case.

I made an appointment to meet my clients at their home early that evening. Moonpie Mountain is a steep hill that sits above Dogstown. The hill has its base on the north side of the shores of the Beaver Butt River, the final bit of high ground before the river meets the sea. The west bottom of Moonpie fades into the town of Dogstown itself. It's a beautiful, rugged, and very prominent piece of real estate, and my clients claim the right as lawful owners of the majority of it. Their house is perched on a small ledge about four hundred feet above the northwest corner. It's tucked back into the towering trees that cover the property, so it's almost invisible from below, but the view from there is worth millions. I had a couple hours before I was to meet them, and since I was on that side of the Butt, I decided to take a quick trip up to Trapper's and pick up my smoked salmon. It might make a nice treat for my clients. Besides, I had finally talked with my mother this afternoon and promised that I'd bring some over for dinner tomorrow.

On the way to Trapper and Roxy's place, I drove past "the Cove," a local surf spot. The swell that had been forecast to arrive was here and pumping in toward shore. There were five or six surfmobiles in the parking area: rusted-out cars and vans that seemed to be held together with bumper stickers. The sound system is usually worth more than the rest of the car. My car is usually there in the lineup, and if I wasn't being responsible, I'd be there with them myself. I was speeding past when I saw Trapper's van coming toward me from the other direction. He had his turn signal on to pull into the surf lot. I waved and hit the brakes, slowed, and did a U-turn. I pulled Prince Valiant into the parking space next to him and got out just as he was climbing from his van.

"Hey, dude, where's your board?" he asked, dragging his nine-foot tri-fin surfboard out of the back his rig.

"I'm actually working," I said both proudly and regrettably. "Actually, I was just on my way up to your house."

"What? You gotta be kidding. These are the nicest waves we've had in a month," he stopped what he was doing and looked at me, totally dumbfounded. "Wait a minute. You? Working?" He came up to me and stuck his face right into mine. "Who are you? What did you do with Duke?" Trapper kind of pushed me aside and went over to my car. In the back seat were a large plastic bin that I keep my wetsuit in and a few empty gallon jugs lying on the floor—I use those as bottles for hot water so I can have a warm shower when I come out of the surf. He turned toward me and grabbed one of my ears and put his other hand on my forehead, then started pulling. I thought he'd yank my face right off my face. "Okay, you! Take off this mask, and tell me what you did with my little buddy!"

"Ow! Trapper! Ow! Leggo!"

He let go of my ear and pushed me backward, laughing. "Well, okay. You must be the real thing. If you were anybody else, you'd be putting up a fight." He chuckled as he went back to the rear of his van. "So I see your wetsuit in there. You can borrow one of my boards for a bit."

"No. I'd love to, but, really, I don't have time. Really, I'm working," I said. "I have to be up to see the Canfields in about an hour. I think I've got their property dispute figured out. I was heading over to your house to grab some of that smoked salmon. I thought I'd share a little bit with them."

"You sure?" he asked. "I've got my eight-six right here." Trapper and I surf with longboards—surfboards that are at least a couple feet longer than we are tall. He's almost a foot taller than I am, so for him a board that's eight and a half feet long—an "eight six"—is his shortest surfboard, but for me it's just about right.

"No thanks," I said. "Besides, that wetsuit's been sitting in that bucket for almost a week. I need to wash it out before I put it on again. Strange things like to grow in dark wet places—who knows what's been breeding in there."

"Okay, but how about tomorrow morning? We can meet out here early, get in a couple rides, then you can go to work. Whatever that is, besides hanging out and flirting with the old ladies at the county."

"Yeah, that sounds good. After I wrap up this case, I won't have much to do for a while. There's a lead on a family dispute, but that can wait. Hopefully something else will come along," I said. "I really don't feel like tailing a couple people who can't decide if they still love each other more than they do the people they're having affairs with. There's a big difference between being a private eye and a peeping tom."

"Well, listen to you. You solve one murder case and now you're too good for the rest of us." By this time, Trapper had gotten into his wetsuit and was locking up his van. "Okay, tomorrow morning." He started down the trail toward the beach.

"Wait!" I shouted after him. "Is Roxy home? What about the smoked salmon?"

"There's a couple bags in the beer fridge in the garage with your name on it. Just take it. It's all yours," he shouted back as he kept walking toward the surfline.

I drove up the bluff to Trapper and Roxy's and parked my car in the driveway. Roxy's car wasn't there—I had the place to myself. I went into the garage, grabbed my smoked salmon, and walked back out to the driveway. The view from their driveway is expansive—you can see out to sea from almost the state line to the south all the way to Port Awful to the north. Port Awful is the next small town north of CatsCamp. It's also one of the few deep-water ports on the Left Coast north of San Franciscan. Boats can get in and out of that port when others are closed due to high surf or big storms.

Looking out over the ocean, I noticed about two dozen fishing boats trolling in a ragged line a mile or so past the whitewater of the surf along shore. I hadn't really paid much attention to boats offshore before, but with my newfound interest in chasing salmon, I became aware of the different size and colors of the crafts. I went to my car and fished my old binoculars out from under the seat. In reality and functionally, they were, in effect, monoculars as one of the lenses had fogged over a few years back after they had taken an accidental swim in my cooler. Inspecting the boats closer, I could really tell the differ-ence between the recreational fishermen and the commer-cial boats. The commercial boats were considerably larger, had more people on board, and had long outriggers hanging off the sides like the arms of a praying mantis. I counted four boats—larger than the others and painted a dark green, almost black—that looked like they were pulling up nets. Were they shrimp boats? I thought it was illegal to net fish this close to shore as the nets scraped along the bottom and effectively denuded the underwater landscape. These four boats were another couple of miles past the other boats. I made a mental note to ask Trapper or Cary about that.

I drove down the hill, back into town, and started the steep climb up Moonpie Mountain. The potholed road, made of crumbling coastal shale, was bouncing me and my car around. The incline making the motor growl and the transmission howl. My poor car pulled into the Canfield's driveway, making some strange noises and emitting funky, burning odors.

The Canfields are a nice elderly couple. Mr. and Mrs. Canfield—they insisted that I call them Pat, her name is Patricia, his is Patrick but I felt silly doing so—are pretty self-sufficient. They were waiting on their front porch looking very Norman Rockwell-ish when I drove up. They introduced me to their small herd of milk goats, showed me a nice orchard of apple and cherry trees, as well as a huge garden with chickens. They want nothing else but to live out their days up on Moonpie.

The developers—a wealthy group of seals from down the Coast—couldn't get the Canfields to accept any offer, reasonable or otherwise. So they tried to cook up some story that said that one of them has a relative from long ago who was the original owner of the property.

However, the paperwork that I found on file at the county tells quite a different story. It's true that one owner from way back when was related to a member of the group, but he lost the deed in a poker game trying to fill a straight flush from the inside out. Not a good investment strategy, I'd say. On top of that, after he lost that hand, he accused the dealer of cheating and went to pull his gun out of his pocket. Another bad move; the gun fired before he could pull it out and he shot himself in the private parts. He survived, but was forever known around the county under his new name, "Juan Ballo."

Pat, Pat, and I laughed about that, ate smoked salmon, and drank a little goat's milk—in my case *very* little. Nasty stuff, maybe because I met the goat it came from. I had brought a bottle of wine, and the three of us put a dent in that bottle watching the sun sink into the sea from their front porch high above the beach.

They sent me home with a little basket of apples, carrots, and goat cheese. They also sent me off with a nice little paycheck. By this time I was feeling pretty good, but pretty beat. It had been a long day, and I couldn't wait to get home, but I took it easy picking my way down through the holes in the gravel road, careful not to bounce out over a corner and down the cliff.

Being so mellow, I didn't notice the pair of headlights slowly closing in on my rearview mirror once I got onto pavement. I wasn't driving too fast, maybe about five miles under the speed limit, so I figured this car was just in more of a hurry than I was. I pulled off the highway and down the street toward my home. The car slowed down as I did. By this time, I was getting a little worried. Except for half a glass of wine, I hadn't had anything to drink and I wasn't speeding, so I rolled down the window to see who it was. As I parked in front of my apartment building, the car slowed down as it approached. The driver, who had a strong resemblance to Deputy Wilson, but not wearing a uniform, gave me the two-fingers-one-finger "I'm looking at you" gesture as it motored slowly past.

CHAPTER 6

Another snoop Job

Wednesday dawned…well to be honest, I have no idea how it dawned. By the time I got up, the sun was already shining down on the Beaver Butt river and from my kitchen window—if I stood on my tiptoes and leaned over the back of the fridge—I could see there were already a couple of boats out trolling around.

I looked in the fridge and saw that there were still five bottles of beer from yesterday, but other than that, nothing substantial for breakfast. I supposed I could have plopped that last pickle in that last tortilla and smeared that stinky last bit of the mayonnaise on it, but I just got paid. A big hot breakfast at Spanky's sounded good.

Then maybe a little surfing, maybe a little fishing, maybe just some catnip and a nap—right? As we say on the feline side of the river, "nip and nap." Why not? I really didn't have anything else going on.

It was just squeakily past eleven o'clock by the time I waddled out the front door of Spanky's and squeezed myself behind Prince Valiant's steering wheel. A word of advice, don't take up the challenge to finish Spanky's Super Fisherman's Special breakfast. Here's the deal: you get a five-egg omelet filled with ham, beef, and half a metric ton of veggies served with two pounds of home fries, a short stack of pancakes, a chocolate milkshake, and a large Bloody Mary. The challenge is that if you finish all of it—every last goopy crumb—in thirty minutes, you don't have to pay for it. I finished it, but not in time. I missed by almost half an hour—hey, I'm a cat. That was pretty close, right?—and had to pay for the whole thing, and now I was so bloated I thought I was going to vomit and then pass out. Hopefully in that order.

Prince had been parked in the sun all morning and was nice and warm—a little stinky as usual, but a pleasant nap-inducing warm. We—Prince and I—rambled out to a little sandy pullout off the coast highway and settled in to watch the tide go out.

I swear it was no more than ten seconds later when I felt my phone buzzing in my pocket. I still have one of the original flip phones. I fumbled for it—taking a picture of the inside of my crotch pocket during the process—and on the other end was my buddy Trapper. "Where the f——k are you?!" he yelled into my still asleep ear. "I've been here since noon—half an hour ago—waiting for you. What the f——k is up with you!"

"I'm not sure. I…uh, think I'm ….uh…" was all I could mumble out of my goopy half-asleep mouth while I squinched my eyes, blinking at the glare off the ocean. "Where are you?"

"I'm at the bait shop. I'm gonna be here for five more minutes," he said pseudo-calmly. And in a total shift of perspective screamed into the phone, *"Get your mangy cat-ass over here!"*

"Dude! Quit shouting. I musta fell asleep. I'm, uh…hmmm… I'll be there in a second. See ya. Bye." I hung up. That dog saves my ass more often that I can blink, but he chews my ass more than anyone besides my mother—and that's a close race.

I must have been asleep for an hour and a half. That was nice, but now I was a little groggy. "Let's see…bait shop. Bait shop. Oh right! I have to replace the gear that went overboard back when the motor stalled," I said aloud while I fired up the car and swung out onto the highway, just missing Mario Andretti at the wheel of a fully loaded log truck coming the other way.

My tires squealed as I skidded into the parking lot of Cary's Tackle Box. Trapper was just reaching for the handle of his van and not looking too happy.

"Dude. If you were canine, I'd kick your ass for making me wait. Since you're a lazy cat who uses a calendar instead of a watch to tell time, all I can do is shake my head." He slapped me on the back of my head and said, "C'mon, let's do this. I already picked out a couple reels for you to look at. Then I gotta go. I've got a life, you know. I can't always be waiting on you."

We walked into the store, and spread out on the back counter were half a dozen fishing reels. Behind them were two nice stout but flexible fishing rods. Behind the counter was Cary, looking much hap-pier than the day before, anticipating a nice sale to start the afternoon. "Well, look who rolled out of bed," he said as we approached the lineup of gear spread out for us to inspect. He and Trapper did most of the talking; I just gave a couple yeses and nos. Before I knew it, Cary was loading fishing line onto two beautiful gold-colored reels while Trapper was leading me over to the racks of hooks, lures, weights, and other fishing gizmos.

I stood there listening but not really hearing as Trapper started pulling stuff off the rack and handing it to me. "You're gonna need a couple of these, four of those, eight of these, a hundred of those, a thousand of these, a million of those…" was what I heard.

"Duke. Duke! Are you even here today? Can you just pay attention for five minutes? I'm here to help you. If you don't want my help, I can go. Okay?"

"All right. Sorry Trap. I was watching those guys. Do we need any of the stuff they're looking at?" At the end of the aisle were two old guys who definitely had some frog lineage, you could tell by their wide mouths and smooth skin. They were picking up, inspecting, and debating the merits of tiny little hooks decorated with brightly colored feathers. I looked at the size of the hooks and things that Trapper was loading me up with and noticed how much bigger and far less ornate my stuff was.

"No, Duke," Trapper said, rolling his eyes. "They're fly fisherman."

"Oh! I get it. That's why their stuff is so tiny. We're fishing for salmon. They're going after flies. What do you do with the flies after you catch them?"

"No, Duke," Trapper said, rubbing the temples on the side of his forehead as if he had suddenly gotten the kind of headache you get when you eat ice cream too fast. "They use artificial bugs to catch fish." Trapper briefly explained to me how fly fishing works, and even though we use different techniques and target different prey, it's still fishing—for fish. "We call that 'fishin' froggie-style,'" Trapper said.

I was interested and moved a little closer to hear what the two old frogs were saying—that's me, the curious cat.

"This looks like a trout magnet, I tell you what," one of them croaked to the other, holding up a chartreuse and magenta shiny piece of fuzz. "My grandson's comin' up ta visit, and we're going out to Meyer's Ditch."

"I heard thet Natural Resources was stocking the ditch with trophy-sized trout this weeken'," the other said.

"Yep. It's 'Take a Kid Fishin' weekend. The little pollywog came up for it last year, and we had a great time," the first one said. "Thet tadpole got inta muh flybox, and durned if he dint et half a dozen before he knew what they were!"

They both started chuckling in the weird way frogs do, sounding more like they were swallowing cups of Jell-O than regular laughing. "Duke! C'mon, let's go," Trapper said, pulling me toward the checkout counter.

As we approached the cash register, a group of otters were talking with Cary. There were three of them, and as I got closer, I recognized them as the ones that gave me a tow a couple days before—basically saving me from a watery grave. They seemed pretty deep in discussion with Cary. I didn't know what to say other than a nod and a smile.

I moved a little nearer and noticed a large cooler splattered with bloodstains. I guess that would seem out of place in other stores, but looking around, I saw guns, ammo, bows and arrows, knives, spears, and I wouldn't be surprised to find a cannon somewhere in there. So a little blood is almost expected. It turns out that they were selling fresh anchovies to Cary for bait. Cary was explaining how business was slow and he still had plenty in the freezer. He offered to take half of what they wanted to sell, and he could only pay three-quarters of what they wanted to get. Both sides of the negotiation looked pretty unhappy over the whole deal. Cary surely wished that business was strong enough to help the otters out, and the otters unquestionably needed the money.

"Hey, Trapper, aren't we gonna need bait?" I asked my buddy a little louder than normal conversation.

Trapper was deeply engrossed in the latest issue of *Women in Waders* magazine. He looked up and said, "Nah. We'll get bait before we go fishing. We don't need it today," and then went back to his magazine.

"Trapper. I think we need to buy some bait," I said, rolling my eyes and gesturing toward the otters. "These are the guys who gave me a tow the other day."

He put down his magazine and smiled at the three. "I don't know whether to thank you guys for saving poor little Duke's life, or if it would have been better just to let him drift out to sea," he said jokingly. At least I'm pretty sure he was joking.

The otters didn't know what to think either. They looked a little confused and a little concerned.

"Hey, I'm just kidding!" Trapper said. He came over, gave me a big bone-crushing hug, and said, "Listen, Duke, you buy all the bait you want. It looks good and fresh. What you're not gonna use in the next couple days, you can just throw in a baggie and freeze it. Okay. You should be all set up now. I'm takin' off. I've already wasted too much daylight in here with you." He headed for the door, saying goodbye to Cary and the otters.

Cary turned to the otters and said, "I'll be right with you guys. Lemme take care of Duke here and we'll see what I can do for you." He started scanning all the rods, reels, line, hooks, weight, lures, and three packages of bait—more than I'll use in six months—and gave me a total. It was a lot more than I expected, but I had just gotten paid so I could afford it. And I did have to replace Butch's rod and reel, so I didn't have much choice. But now I'm going to have drum up another gig pretty soon. So much for a month of being a lazy cat.

The three otters stood silently watching and waiting as I finished paying and taking an armload of stuff to my car. When I returned for the rest of my purchase, they were all talking together quietly. I couldn't quite carry everything left in one trip, so Cary offered to carry the remainder out to my car with me, but one of the otters stepped forward and said, "No, Mr. Cary. I will help. Let me get that, Mr. Duke."

"Oh. Hey, that's great. I appreciate it. What's your name again?"

"I never told you my name," he said, handing me a box of assorted gear.

I waited a while, and he still didn't say anything. "So what *is* your name?" I asked.

"Down here I'm called John. Upriver my name is different. You call me John," he said with a shy smile.

By this time, the other two otters had come outside, carrying their cooler of bait. They seemed a little less disappointed than they were inside. Maybe my big purchase helped Cary take some of their bait off their hands.

"Did you ask? Is he going to do it?" one of them asked John. John turned to them and said, "I not ask yet. Have patience."

"What are you guys talking about?" I asked. "Am I supposed to be doing something for you? Look, you three saved my life. I owe you a favor. What do you need?"

"There are very bad things happening upriver," John said. "Our friend Scottie was murdered on Saturday. The police won't bother with it. They say it was an accident, that he was drinking and driving his boat on the river at night."

"Yeah! He might have been nobody to Sheriff, but he was brother to us!" one of the others said. "He was a good husband and father. Now there is a widow and two pups with no dad to raise them the right way."

"Mr. Duke," John said. "We have no money, but we are good fisherman. All cats like fish. Mr. Cary says you are very good ace private eye. You find out who killed Scottie. We pay you all the fish you want for a year."

I looked at their bloody, beat-up cooler full of sardines and anchovies. It would take a lot of those minnows to make a meal. The otters knew what I was thinking.

"No. No. Mr. Duke, this just bait. Come over here." They led me to a rusted old station wagon that was probably wider than most cars are long these days. In the back of the car was another cooler in pretty much the same shape as both the car and the first cooler. They opened it up, and it was full of salmon fillets and freshly cooked Dungeness crab legs. It looked delicious. Because of agreements with the government from the days when the otters' lands were taken from them and they were relocated to reservations, the otters are exempt from laws that the rest of us have to obey. That cooler full of fish would be cooked and on the plates tonight at restaurants around town by dinnertime.

"We have no money, but we are good fisherman," John said, grinning proudly.

"Okay. John, how about this? I will check it out and let you know in a day or two. Let me snoop around and see what I can find. Sound good?"

The three of them nodded enthusiastically. Each one came up to me and gave me a vigorous—painfully vigorous—handshake.

"Okay. I will meet you here in two days—right here—and let you know what I've found out. Okay? I'm not promising anything, but I'll see what I can find."

The three of them climbed into the front seat of the old station wagon—there was no room anywhere else in the car—and they motored off toward the nicer part of Dogstown, where the fancy restaurants are.

I walked back into the Tackle Box and up to Cary, who was reading the same magazine that Trapper had. "So, Cary, what exactly did you tell those guys? They seem to think that I'm some sort of super-sleuth or something."

Cary looked up and grinned, his teeth stained from those little sweet cigars that he's always smoking. "Well, Duke. I've been in the retail business for quite a long time. Over the years, I've learned how to read people. When I gave you the total for all the stuff that Trapper dumped on the counter for you to buy, well, let's just say that if you looked up the phrase 'sticker shock' in the dictionary, your picture would be right there. I figured that you could use the work, so I told them how you singlehandedly solved the Doggie Crunchies murder case. I didn't lie, I just stretched some facts and left a couple others out. They were quite impressed, weren't they?"

"Apparently so," I said. "You know they have no money. They're going to pay me in fish."

"Duke, those otters consistently catch the most and the best fish. They've been having a tough time of it lately, though. When the fishing's bad, for most people it affects their vacation or their weekend. If the otters don't catch fish, their family goes hungry. And I don't have to tell you that the fishing's been slow lately. You're basically the only real customer I've had all week. Something's going on, on the river. Maybe you can find out what—for them and for me."

"Oh, all right. You're better than slinging guilt around than a jewfish grandmother," I said. "So what can you tell me about the one who died?"

"Well, the dead guy was known to be a bit of a troublemaker, but all in all, he was a good otter, a good husband, and a good dad with a wife and a couple of pups. Upriver he was called Sculpin-boy," Cary said. "He drank a wee bit and liked to fish at night, so the authorities—it happened out of town, so it's under the jurisdiction of the county sheriff—are dismissing it as an unfortunate boating accident. As a matter of fact, they're kind of publicizing the incident as an example of what could happen if you aren't a safe and sober, law-abiding, in-your-bed-at-dark citizen."

CHAPTER 7

Well, That Seals It

Wednesday

Later that afternoon, I got a call from Leo that my boat—yes, *my* boat—was all ready to pick up. I figured that Faye would prob-ably be still at the *Distorter*, so I told him that I'd be right over. I kinda wanted to get back on the Butt and play with my new fishing stuff. In surfing and windsurfing, I was never much of a "Gear Queer." I was always satisfied with whatever worked—no matter how old or ugly—but this fishing stuff was fun to fool with. And yeah, I thought a little time on the water would be good for me and give me time to think about the otter's proposal.

I got the boat. Leo didn't even charge me. Apparently Faye came back on cloud nine, and that was good enough for him. I'm gonna hafta talk with Faye. First Ginger, now Leo. I don't know what she's telling them, but I got the feeling that it ain't exactly what it looks like from my side of the mirror.

I drove back into CatsCamp, down to the public boat ramp, and put the boat in the bay. *Myrtle*? No. If it's gonna be my boat, it's gotta have a cool name. And definitely not *Myrtle*. I decided that I'm going to rename her as the…um…*Steelhead Slayer*. Yeah, that's a good name.

I put the *Steelhead Slayer* in and motored out into the bay, feeling pretty cool. I baited my new rod, and after dropping my offering into the water, I got in line with the other trollers. After about half an hour of not even a nibble, I heard a loud engine noise coming from the Dogstown side of the river. Two large black—I mean *flat* black—boats came charging out of the Dogstown marina. One—the smaller of the two—turned right and headed upriver. I didn't get a good look at the boat, except that it was a jet drive—made to handle the shallow shoals and riffles. There were three people in the boat. The second boat—a little larger than the other—was a deep-vee with a propel-ler drive, and it was charging right toward the fleet of boats trolling for salmon in the bay—one of which was me! It was moving fast. The other fishermen were frantically reeling in their lines and heading toward shore as if this was a usual occurrence. Me? I didn't know what to do, so I did what the others were doing. I put the boat into neutral, pulled my pole out of the rod holder, and started reeling in. Before I knew it, the black boat was almost on top of me. At first I thought he didn't see me, but as it came bearing down, it looked like he was deliberately aiming for me. I was still reeling in my line when the boat steered slightly to starboard and just barely missed me. His bow wake rocked the *Steelhead Slayer* so hard it knocked me painfully hard into the side of my boat and almost capsized me. By the time I stood back up, I could only see the large back transom as it bulled through the line of breakers at the river's mouth. There were four people on board. Two of them were looking back at me and laughing. They looked like the same four that were having lunch at Spanky's.

I motored *The Slayer* back to the CatsCamp boat ramp and tied her off on the dock while I went up to get Prince Valiant and the trailer. I backed down the ramp and hooked the boat up. After I had gotten up off the ramp and was in the parking lot, rinsing her off and tying her down, putting my fishing gear away, and getting ready to drive the quarter mile to my apartment, another fisherman pulled in next to me to do the same thing. Two old cats got out of the truck towing a nice new jet boat still dripping wet.

"Well, if it isn't the ol' *Myrtle*. I thought that boat had finally sunk for the last time," the driver said.

"Actually, the boat's name is *The Steelhead Slayer*," I replied. "*Myrtle* just didn't do it for me."

"What? That's crazy. You *never* rename a boat—especially one with as much history as the ol' *Myrtle*," the other one said, climbing up the trailer and into the boat. He picked up a large white plastic cooler and handed it down to the driver. "That's bad luck, fer sher. It's as bad as eating bananas."

"Bananas? What d'you mean?" I asked.

"C'mon. Really? Everyone knows that you can't catch a fish if you've got bananas on board. And really—renaming a boat is just asking for trouble," the driver said. He opened up the cooler and pulled out a large silvery salmon. The two of them started walking toward the fish cleaning station.

Hmmmm, I thought to myself. *Bananas. Who woulda thunk it? Okay. No bananas, but the name is changing. Maybe I better ask Trapper what he thinks.* I finished strapping down the *Slayer*—love that name—and headed home. I backed the trailer into the driveway, taking up my only parking spot. I parked at the curb, grabbed my new rod and reel and tackle box out of the boat, and went inside to listen to my grumbling stomach and stare at my empty fridge.

"Maybe I'll head up to Moleknuckle for dinner," I said aloud. "I haven't eaten at the Poison Oak in a while." The Poison Oak is a restaurant upriver that in the summer catered to visitors taking the jet boat excursions from Dosgtown as well as the occasional fish-er-man, but this time of year it was a local's hangout. Maybe I could find out a little bit about Scottie and why someone wanted him dead. It's not an easy drive to Moleknuckle—the road is always buckling in some places, sections of it are gravel, and long stretches are single lane with steep cliffs on either side. In Prince Valiant, I aver-age about twenty-five miles per hour, which means it takes thirty-six minutes to drive the fifteen miles—if my math is correct. Whatever. The Poison Oak has a restaurant side and a bar side. I looked around the restau-rant side and saw that only one table was occupied. There was an older canine woman sitting there by herself. She looked to be of some terrier lineage—probably Schnauzer—with short gray wiry hair. She was wearing some odd-looking uniform—a tight offi-cial-looking tan shirt that had an emblem of some organization sewn on the shoulder, medium-length brown skirt, tan socks that came halfway up her shins, and sensible brown shoes. She also wore a frown, and she wore it professionally. I took a stroll around the room pretending to look for a table so I could get a closer look at whose uniform she was wearing.

As I approached, she looked up at me and said sternly, "Yes? What do you want?" as if I was there to question her. "Um… uh…nothing. I was just looking for a seat with a nice view," I stammered. Actually you couldn't find a seat in the dining room that *didn't* have a nice view. Floor-to-ceiling windows looked out through a forest of old-growth firs down a gentle slope covered in moss and fern to an expansive rockbar fronting a series of rapids of the middle Beaver Butt river. There was a flat black jet boat beached on the rockbar, its bow line tied off to one of the large firs.

"Maybe I'll check the lounge," I said. I didn't get a good chance to see what kind of uniform she was wearing, but it certainly wasn't the Sheriff's Department nor the Tribal Police. I walked into the bar, and it was strikingly different than the open and naturally lit dining room. The place was small, dark, cramped, and kind of musty. It was a narrow room with the bar along one side, some small tables along the other, and a pool table in the middle. The only light came from neon beer signs, the lamp over the pool table, and the blue glow of a television. Sitting at the far end of the bar were three seals. I took the stool closest to the door—just in case—and farthest from the seals— also just in case. The bartender came over, and I ordered a bottle of Drab Light. She brought it to me with a nice cold glass and a smile. She was a pretty young otter with bright blue eyes and light curly hair that cascaded down her back to the top of her cute little behind.

"Surprised to see seals this far upriver," I said to her quietly. "Yeah. They've been hanging around these past couple months.

They're okay. They keep to themselves and pay their tab," she replied softly. "Just don't provoke 'em. I think they *like* to fight. They do it a lot."

"Okay," I whispered back. "I'll be good." Leaning back and taking a long sip off my beer, I said in a louder voice, "Sorry to hear about Scottie. I mean, it's so sad with his young family and all."

At the mention of the word *Scottie*, the seals' heads snapped around to stare directly at me. *Whoops*, I thought, remembering the bartender's words, "they *like* to fight."

"Hey! Who are you?" one of them snarled at me. He looked to be the leader of the gang—bigger, stockier, and definitely the alpha personality.

"Me? I'm nobody. I'm just passing through and having a beer. Really. I'm nobody. Honest," I said, trying to hide behind my beer. My sick sixth sense was tingling. I could feel my hair starting to stand on end and my back starting to arch. It's a feline thing.

"It is only an otter, not like it was one of us, you know," he said to me, getting off his barstool and starting slowly toward me. The other two stood up but didn't move. "Just passing through, eh? This is the end of the road, cat—in many more ways than you know. If I were you, I wouldn't bother finishing that beer. I would just turn around and head back downstream and keep your little cat nose out of seal business." He kept walking toward me slowly. "As a matter of fact, *cat*,"—he spat out the word *cat* as if it tasted of soap (obviously a foreign substance to this particular seal, I realized the closer he got to me)—"I think you should keep your whole *self* out of Moleknuckle. Why don't you go back downstream where someone like you might not get hurt? It can be awfully dangerous up here in these woods. Right, boys?"

"Right," I said quickly. "That's just what I'm gonna do. Right. Here I go." I ran out of there so quickly I tripped on the doorstep and rolled out into the gravel driveway. I could hear the laughter of three stinky seals coming from the barroom door as I picked myself up with as much dignity as I could assemble and calmly walked to my car.

I stood outside my car, wondering if it would be safe to back to the dining room. Between those seals and that Schnauzer, it didn't seem like such a good idea, but I was still hungry and this was the only place with food within forty minutes. While I was standing there, the bartender came out and shouted across the lot to me, "Hey, cat. You still owe for that beer!"

The laughter coming from behind her increased in both volume and intensity.

Right then the big, old rusty station wagon full of otters and coolers that was at Cary's pulled in next to me. John got out and vigorously shook my hand—again a little too vigorously.

"Hello, Mr. Duke. You are here working on the case. That is good," he said.

"Well, not exactly. I'm still checking things out. I'm not too sure I want to get in the middle of this," I lied. It was too late. In my mind, I was already in the middle of this. "I'm still doing preliminary research," I added, trying to sound professional.

John looked me up and down. "Are you okay, Mr. Duke? You have gravel in your hair. Did you fall?" He squinted and looked me squarely in the eyes. "The seals are in the bar, yes? Did they do anything?" With that, he turned to the other two and gave them a quick wink and head shake. The other two nodded and started for the barroom door. "We go talk to them for you."

"No, wait," I said quickly. "I don't want any trouble. It's fine." I handed John a ten-dollar bill. "But if you can pay my tab for me, that'd be great. I left before I could take care of that."

John kept squinting at me.

"If there's anything left, get yourself one, too," I added. "I need to get back down to CatsCamp for a…an important meeting."

Still squinting, John came closer until his face was just inches from mine. "We go fishing together. More research. You meet me at Limprock boat ramp tomorrow morning. Sunrise. We catch some fish. We talk where nobody hears."

I left there a little confused. Ursalik, just the day before, had said it was a murder. These guys were saying that the people in charge were now spinning it in a different direction. Something smelled a little fishy.

CHAPTER 8

A Block in the Road

I got up early the next morning. It was Thursday. My stomach was rolling from the night before. After I left Moleknuckle, I went to the Stump and Grind, but the kitchen was closed. Marge nuked a nasty rat burrito for me, and I washed it down with another a beer. Not exactly what one would call a gourmand feast, but it was better than nothing—not by much, but still better than going to bed hungry.

I looked at my phone. No messages, but it was already 5:45, and I had to be upriver in fifteen minutes. I jumped into a pair of jeans, slid into an old sweatshirt, fell into my flip-flops, and headed out the door.

"Oh right!" I said out loud, remembering where I was going and what I was doing. I raced back inside and grabbed my pole and tackle box. I threw my fishing gear in the back seat and tore outta there.

Limprock Memorial Campground is a nice place. It's about ten miles up the Butt from CatsCamp, the perfect distance from the ocean and about halfway to Moleknuckle. There are about fifty campspots, each with electric hookups and fire pits. During the summer, it's packed with families either from the coast, coming up to get away from the cold wind off the ocean, or from further inland, escaping the summer swelter. In addition to the campsites, there is a paved boat ramp to give folks access to the river. A lot of fishermen use Limprock as a base when fishing upriver. It's freshwater, so you don't need to rinse the salt from your engine and trailer at the end of the day, and there's a large fish cleaning station there as well.

I drove through the campground and down onto the rockbar. I got there at 6:01. *Not bad*, I thought. For a feline, being on time is being early. Canines have a different view where being right on time means you're late, but personally, I was impressed with my punctuality.

I parked Prince Valiant off to the side, underneath some over-hanging scratchberry vines so it would be out of the way of people using the ramp. Nobody else was there. It was still kinda dark. The sun was just coming up. It was chilly. Everything was wet from dew. All was quiet except for the occasional splash of a kingfisher hitting the water and the squawk of a blue jay waking up his neighbors. The sky was turning rosy pink to the east and lightening up to a clear royal blue to the west. This far upriver, there is no coastal fog—it was going to be a hot and sunny Indian summer day.

"I'm looking forward to being on the river up here. It'll be much nicer than trolling around in the cool damp windy fog in the bay," I said aloud to the scrub jay screeching at me from his perch in an alder tree across the river.

I saw some small fish rising to try and snag a stray mosquito and decided that since I was there and had my fishing gear, I should try and catch something. The problem was that all my lures and hooks and even my line were meant for catching big salmon down in the bay. My first cast splashed right where the little fish were hunting. It scared them all away. However, I didn't realize that and kept casting away. After about twenty minutes of casting practice—you couldn't call it fishing—my reel revolted on me and left me with a rat's nest of monofilament.

"Awww shit!" I said.

I walked back up to my car and started to untangle and unravel the mess on my rod.

Where is John? I wondered. He didn't seem like the kind of guy that would stand me up. He was pretty adamant that we were fishing together this morning. Actually it was pretty quiet all around, I didn't even hear any cars on the road. Just then I *did* hear something, actually a couple things. First, I heard a boat—sounded like a jet boat—coming down river. Then I heard another boat—also a jet—approaching from downriver. I threw my rod and my mess of a reel into the back seat and crouched down behind my car. Something didn't feel right, and I wanted to watch without being watched.

The sun was coming up, but it still wasn't fully light out. The boat coming from upriver rounded the bend above the boat ramp. It was black—a matte black that was the color of a moonless night. It looked like the same boat that was moored on the rockbar below the Poison Oak yesterday. The boat approaching from downstream appeared to be a carbon copy of the other—black and fast. The two boats converged on the boat ramp at the same time a truck came through the campground and down the ramp. It wasn't the kind of truck that a fisherman would drive. It was a small square boxy truck—more of a cargo delivery van. On top of that, it had no boat on a trailer behind it. Why was it backing down the boat ramp? I moved around my car to get a better look.

It was painted to look like a phone company truck. The two boats pulled up to shore with a crew of three seals in each. The seals unloaded large black coolers into the back of the truck silently and quickly—I could tell by the choreographed movements that this was not the first time they've done this. I could see gill nets with their floats painted black in the stern of the two boats. The whole unloading process took less than four minutes, and then the boats dispersed. The truck pulled away, and I thought I recognized the driver from one of the city or county offices, but I couldn't quite place him in the dawn's early light.

Scarcely two minutes later, John and the other otters showed up at the ramp. "Sorry to be so late," John said, climbing out of the station wagon. Behind the car on a rusty trailer was a beat-up alumi-num fishing boat. It had a squared-off bow, a large outboard engine, and not much else. It was a jet-sled with no comforts—purely made for catching fish. "We were stuck behind some road construction coming up from town. We had to get bait. They said that there was a rockslide blocking the road and they had to clear it."

"Hmmm…I drove up that road less than an hour ago and didn't see any rockslide," I told him. "I guess I'm lucky that it didn't happen when I was coming through."

John squinted at me—he seems to do that a lot—and said, "You do not believe me? I do not lie."

"No," I replied. "Of course I believe you." Changing the subject, I said, "So did you see that phone company truck that just left? Apparently he made it through the rockslide." While the other two were launching the boat, I told John about the two boats and the truck and the coolers.

John continued squinting and said quietly, looking around as if the trees had ears, "I saw the truck and know those seals. They are stealing fish. They throw their nets out at night. We complain to the county, but nothing happens."

CHAPTER 9

Upriver Death Threats

We fished that morning and into the afternoon. We caught a couple nice steelhead trout and talked quite a bit about seals and otters. There has always been more than just bad blood between the two groups. They share some common beliefs on religion, worshipping the Earth Mother as opposed to any unseen and arbitrarily ruthless god, but other than that, the two couldn't be more different mainly in terms of honesty. Otters believe strongly that to be untruthful is a crime against everyone, and they mean *everyone* living, dead, or still unconceived. Seals, on the other hand, don't care if what they say is true as long as it furthers their agenda. Otters are smaller than seals, cleaner, have stronger family bonds, and are more fun-loving. By tradition, the males all get nicknames when they go through puberty. The female otters get names at birth, but take their husband's name when they marry. The seals have always been bullies to the otters. The history of the two is laced full of unsolved disap-pearances. Along with fishing, John also gave me a short tour of the Beaver Butt River between Limprock and Moleknuckle. It was gor-geous, huge firs and oaks right down to the river's edge, no houses, no roads. At times it felt like I could have been the first human to ever be there, but John was continually pointing out different points of interest, sites where battles had taken place in the days before the canines and felines showed up, places where his ancestors had lived and loved. We motored up to one particular rockbar, and we all got out of the boat. The three otters knelt down before a large rock cairn for a couple minutes then got up and solemnly, silently got back in the boat.

"That is where we found Scottie," John said as we started gliding downriver. Not much was said for the remainder of the trip.

At Limprock, I helped the otters load the boat onto the trailer. We put the cooler with the fish in the back of the station wagon. As I was walking to my car determined to drive back home, have some catnip, and flop onto my couch, John leaned out of the station wagon window and said, "You come to my home for dinner tonight. We eat salmon and talk." After he said that, the three of them drove away.

That's thing I was beginning to learn about John. He doesn't ask—he tells. He didn't ask if I wanted to have dinner at his house, he simply told me that I was. I didn't know where he lived, and before I could ask, he was gone. Don't get me wrong, I like the guy—even more so after the day on the river. He really is genuinely a very nice, brutally honest, and caring person, and I really felt that if I could help him out, I needed to. Something about karma or something. Who knows?

After my little nip and nap, I drove up to Moleknuckle but didn't know where to start looking for John. I thought I could spot that big ugly car of his, but didn't see it anywhere so I went to the Poison Oak. Maybe that cute little bartender could tell me how to get to his house.

I slowly opened the door to the barroom and was relieved to see that the seals were not there. Thankfully, neither was that weird lady in the uniform. For some odd reason, she creeped me out. Just thinking of her made me shudder. The lovely bartender was the only one there. She was sitting on a bar stool watching some game show on the small television above the freezer that was used for chilling glasses. When she saw me come in, she changed the channel to a batball game. She opened up a bottle of Drab Light and pulled a glass out of the freezer. She placed the glass and bottle in front of me.

"It's about time you got here. My brother said you'd be coming in," she said. "That'll be four bucks. You're not running out on your tab again. C'mon, pay up."

I just stood there not knowing what to say. Usually in cir-cum-stances like this, some smart-alecky cat remark will just flow off my tongue, but this gal had me spellbound. So much to take in all at once—not only how utterly attractive she was, but her brother told her to expect me, and she didn't seem to care that those seals were ready to skin me alive yesterday. She remembered what my beer of choice is, but wanted to make sure that she got paid for it. My head was spinning.

"And just who is your brother?" I asked, thinking, *Okay, let's clear up that mystery first.*

"Four bucks," she said.

"Okay, okay." I pulled out a fiver and slapped it on the bar. She took it and put it in the register. She pulled a single out of the drawer and put it in a jar next to the freezer.

"Do I get change?" I asked. "No."

"All right then, consider that your tip," I said, smiling. "I did."

"So, again, who is your brother?" I asked again.

"You know. Don't be stupid with me. Stupid ain't cute."

"Hmmph. So what's *your* name then?"

"I'm Willamina," she said, extending her right hand over the bar. "Nice to meet you, Duke. Finish your beer and let's get out of here."

"Wha…what?" This was getting weird, but kind of exciting—in a weird way, of course. But if she wanted to, who was I to argue? "And where are we going?" I asked her with a sideways leering glance as I chugged the remains of my pale stale ale.

"I told you. Don't be stupid with me. We're going to my broth-er's for dinner."

"Ahhh…so you're John's sister!"

She rolled her eyes and said, "Really, Duke? He said that you were some genius detective. I'm having a hard time believing the 'genius' part."

Before I could conjure up a snappy comeback, she turned off the television and the lights. Thankfully she opened the door, which let in enough light so I could see my way around.

"C'mon, Duke! Would you *please* hurry up? I'm hungry, and if we're late, my brothers will eat my dinner. Come on! Let's go!"

I hurried to catch up with her, which wasn't easy. By the time I did, she was already at my car. She sat down in the passenger seat just as I was getting behind the wheel.

"Damn, cat. It stinks in here." She was frantically rolling her window down and gasping out of it.

"Sorry," was all I was able to say. "So how do we get there?" She gave me directions, and we managed to get there just as dinner was being served. Round the table were John, Willamina, their three brothers—Bill, Joe, and Dave—and me. Nobody spoke during dinner—they were all concentrating on eating as quick as they could. It was more of a race than a meal. As soon as the food was gone, they all pushed back from the table and belched loudly, followed by roars of laughter. It may have been one of the weirdest dinners I've ever been part of.

Willamina and Bill started clearing the table. John, Joe, Dave and I went out onto the back porch. The sun had already set, and the sky was slowly turning from a fiery red to a deep purple.

"You know that Willamina thinks you're kinda cute, right?" Joe asked.

"Really? Well, she's nice. I like her, too," I said.

"But," Joe continued. "if you ever do *anything* to hurt her in *any* way, one of us will kill you."

"Um…okay," I stammered. "Don't worry. I won't do anything. I promise." What is it with Moleknuckle? This was the second time in two days that I've been threatened with my life.

"So, okay." I turned to John. John was the oldest and obviously the guy in charge of the family. "Well, I've decided that I will take the case. There are too many strange coincidences, and I want to help you. You're good people."

John squinted at me and softly said, "Good." There was a long silent pause.

"Well, okay then. I guess I'm gonna head home," I said. By this time Bill and Willamina had joined us on the porch. All five of them shook my hand—and they all squeezed so hard I thought my arm would fall off.

I drove back down the road alongside the river toward town and home. By that time, it was dark. I could see headlights coming toward me from a ways away, so I crossed the centerline once in a while when I knew there was no oncoming traffic. And at that time of the night at that time of the year, there was not much traffic at all. Actually I was almost back into town before I saw another car, and the one I did see was coming up behind me. It wasn't closing in. It stayed back a nice safe distance. After about a mile of him follow-ing me and me crossing into the other lane, all of a sudden the car behind me closed the gap and was right off my rear bumper. Before I knew it, red-and-blue flashing lights from the roof of the car behind me filled the interior of Prince Valiant. I was getting pulled over. A county sheriff walked up to my rolled-down window. He was a tall feline, about my age, and looked relatively friendly.

"License, registration, and proof of insurance please, sir," the cop said. As I handed him the documents, he wrinkled his nose. He flashed his flashlight around the inside of my car. "Something die in there? What stinks so bad?"

"Sorry, Officer, just some old wetsuits, fish bait, and fast-food wrappers."

The officer, still scanning the papers, looked me in the eye and said, "I recognize you. You're that private investigator cat always snooping around the sheriff's office."

"Yes, sir. That's me."

"Matthew Hazzard. Hmmm…any relation to Duke? My wife is always talking about a Duke Hazzard."

"Yes, sir, that's me. Who's your wife?"

"Her name is Bridgette. She works in the clerk's office."

"Oh! You're Bob! Yeah, Bridgette talks about you, too. All good things. You've got a great wife there," I said. "But she said that you were reassigned to the south end of the county."

"I was, but I lobbied to work closer to home. So now I'm work-ing here, but they gave me the graveyard shift. I get home when Bridge goes to work, and I go to work when she gets home."

"Sounds like Ursalik has it out for you."

He shook his head and said, "It's not Ursalik. He's just following orders from the new city manager. Apparently I'm 'too nice' for my job. They want young toughs like that new guy, Wilson."

"Yeah, I've met him. Kind of a badge-happy jerk if you ask me." Bob smiled with that kind of smile that said he agrees, but can't comment. He handed back my papers and said, "Okay, Duke, I'm gonna let you off with a warning. Stay on your side of the road. Let the Highway Department straighten out the corners, not you."

CHAPTER 10

Who Let the Cat Out?

Friday

The next morning was another gorgeous autumn morning. I love this time of year—bright and sunny and everything shim-mering from dew as if the whole world had just gotten rinsed off. I went into Dogstown and into the county offices. I wanted to check on the legalities of using gill nets on the river. I poked my head into the clerk's office and said hello to Bridgette.

"I met your better half last night," I said. "Bob's a nice guy."

Bridgette looked up from her work and said with a smile and a tinge of sarcasm, "Yeah, he told me he pulled you over for swerving out of your lane. You weren't drinking and driving, were you?"

"No. No. I hadn't had anything to drink. I was up in Moleknuckle visiting with some clients."

"Be careful up there, Duke. There's some dangerous people up that way."

"Don't I know it! I gotta get down to the county counsel's office and check on a couple things. See ya later. Say hi to Bob for me."

I headed down the hall and into the office of the attorney for the county. The county counsel was a stuffy old fox who spent more time on the golf course than in his office. He had two paralegals—

one feline, the other canine—who did all his work for him. He'd show up at important meetings or hearings or whatever and take all the credit for their due diligence—if he won the case. If he lost, it was the two gals who took the blame. Seeing as it was a nice day, I figured that the boss wouldn't be in and I could just deal with his staff.

"Good morning, ladies," I said as I walked in. Behind the counter were the two paralegals—Joy, the feline, and Roze, the canine. Standing in front of the counter was Faye. The three of them looked up from a large hard-cover bound book. It was the County Ledger of Record from four years ago.

Joy held up one finger, then pointed that same finger to a pair of folding chairs sitting in the corner and said, "We'll be with you in a minute, Duke. Have a seat."

As I was sitting in the hard steel chair, Faye turned around, completely ignoring or forgetting what the three of them had been working on and started coming toward me. "Well, hellooo, Dukie," she purred as she sat in the chair next to me.

"Yeah. Hi, Faye," I said. "Please don't call me Dukie. Right? We've talked about this."

"Faye, are we through here? I thought you were trying to find the details of that decision on paving the road to Moleknuckle and the Limprock ramp," Roze said.

Faye looked at her and frowned, then at me and smiled. "Oh that? Yeah, I think I got what I needed," she said, not taking her eyes off me and putting her hand on my thigh.

I jumped up and went to the counter. "So, okay," I said, feeling like I had just been rescued. "I need to know what the rules on gill netting are."

Faye had followed me up to the counter and now had put her arm inside mine. "Ooh…are you working on a case, Dukie? Oh. Sorry. I mean, Duke. This is *so* exciting!"

I pushed her arm back to where it belonged—not in mine— and said, "I'm just doing a little bit of research for a friend, Faye. Now if you don't mind, I need to talk with Joy and Roze."

Faye smiled, winked at me, and went and sat back down in one of the cold uncomfortable metal chairs. "Right. Gotcha. Research. Okay. I'll wait here for ya," she said in some conspiratorial tone.

I turned back to the two gals on the other side of the counter, rolled my eyes, and shook my head. Joy was just coming out from the back room with another huge book.

"Everything about county fishing and angling regulations is in here," she said, dropping the tome on the countertop. It must have weighed forty pounds—at least a quarter of that was dust.

After a few minutes of finding the right section and code, it turns out that at certain times of the year, both the seals and the otters have the right to use gill nets as proscribed by an ancient treaty when the canines and felines "discovered" this territory. Only the seals and otters—no canine, feline, fox, weasel, nor anyone else. However, this was not one of those times. The gillnetting season is very limited and even more regulated. It's only for four days in the early spring and three days in the late fall, only during daylight hours, and only in certain sections of the river. What the seals were doing was very illegal. In addition, netting at night is not only illegal, it is considered to be against any rules of nature and all tenets of religion, beyond blasphemy. Maybe Scottie knew something. Now I know. It got Scottie killed—I was sure of it. Hopefully it wouldn't get me the same.

I said thank you to the two behind the counter and turned to leave. Oh yeah. Faye. She was sitting patiently waiting for me.

"Okay. Now what, Duke?" She said *Duke* as if she was merely shortening the word *Dukie*. "Gillnetters? Let's go get 'em! This is *so* exciting!" She followed me out the door and into the hallway.

"Listen, Faye. This is something I am working on. *I*, not *we*. When the time comes to make this public, you will be the first person to know. In the meantime, I need you to keep this secret. If word gets out"—I lowered my voice and looked from side to side to make sure nobody was listening—"I could be in trouble. Big trouble. So shhh, right?"

Faye's eyes got wide open as if she had just discovered something of her own, then they narrowed down to slits. She looked from side to side and made a motion across her lips like she was zipping her mouth closed and turned her hand as if she was locking her mouth closed, then she made a motion as if she was dropping the key down the front of her blouse. "My lips are sealed and locked, Dukie, but you can come get the key anytime." She winked and walked back into the counsel's office.

I shuddered but managed to say "Okay, thanks, Faye."

As the door closed behind her, I heard her saying, "That's my boyfriend, and he's working on a very dangerous case…"

I opened the door and said aloud to the two paralegals who were seemingly amused by all of this, "I am *not* her boyfriend—we're just friends, that's all—and she's not supposed to say anything to anybody about my…um…research project." I glared at Faye, who was simply smirking back at me. "Right, Faye? Sealed and locked, right?"

"Oh. Right. Gotcha, boss," she said, nodding and winking. "And I'm not your boss, either!" I slammed the door behind me, just imagining what those three females were saying about me now.

I walked out of the county office building into the glaring autumn sunlight. The building is 'bout five blocks from the ocean, and I could hear the waves pounding from that far away. Hmmm…I don't have anything to do for a while. Maybe I should check the surf. I drove down to the Jetty—the closest surf spot. A few decades ago, the Army Engineer Core built two long rock jetties at the mouth of the Beaver Butt River to keep it open year round. Before the jetties, the mouth would be a moving target sometimes way to the south, sometimes a mile or so north and would always be filling with sand. The jetties has kept the Butt's mouth under control. Maybe I need jetties for *my* mouth. But the jetties have also made the area on either side perfect little surf spots, protected from the wind with a back eddy current that makes it easier to get out through the breakers.

Before I even got down there, I could tell that the forecasted swell had arrived in full force. It was way too big for me to even attempt to paddle out, but it was captivating to watch and feel the force of the ocean. Smooth glassy wave faces stood fifteen feet in the air before crashing down. As I stood on the south jetty look-ing at the waves, that large black boat that I had seen a couple of days earlier approached from out at sea. It slowed as it neared the line of towering surf, picked a direction, and sped up. It drove right in between two huge waves, cresting the one in front of it just as it broke into a twelve-foot high mass of whitewater. I watched as it sped through the calm waters between the jetty and veer right toward the Dogstown marina.

I hustled back to my car and drove over to the post office, which is adjacent to the marina. From my vantage point of relative ano-nymity, I could see the boat pull up to a dock near the parking lot. As the boat arrived at the dock, I saw that phone company truck pull up. I pulled out my binoculars to get a clearer picture. The driver of the truck climbed out of the cab and went around to the back. He opened the rear door just as the three seals from the boat arrived with two large coolers. They put the coolers into the back of the truck, the driver closed the door, he got back in the cab, and the three seals went back down the dock to their boat. The driver of the truck was canine and looked to be pretty tall and muscular, but not somebody that I recognized. The truck pulled out of the marina and got onto the coastal highway, heading north toward Port Awful. I had nothing else to do, so I started following it. Maybe, just maybe, this could answer some questions for me. I followed about fifty yards behind the truck for a couple miles when from out of nowhere, a county patrol car pulled up behind me with its lights flashing. I pulled over, not thinking that it was after me, but was on its way to something important up north—like maybe a fire sale at the doughnut shop or something. But no! When I pulled over, it pulled in behind me.

The door opened, and out came Deputy Joe Wilson. "Great," I said aloud. "Now what?"

"Driver's license, registration, and proof of insurance…oh, it's *you* Hazzard. Get out of the car."

"What? Why? What did I do?"

"You were following that truck too closely. I'm taking you in for reckless endangerment."

"What? That's crazy! I was way behind him. How could you tell anyway? You were way behind me." I stayed in my car.

He reached down and put his hand on his service revolver. "The driver is my brother, and he phoned in a complaint. When I pulled behind you, I ran your license plate number and saw that you had gotten pulled over last night. Having to answer to the authorities twice in less than twenty-four hours—reckless endangerment."

"You're making that up. There's no such thing."

"Tell it to the judge, cat. Now get out. We're going downtown."

"No. I'm not getting out. I'll follow you to town, and we can talk to the judge or to Ursalik, or the mayor, or whoever."

"I've called for backup, cat. You can wait in your car if you want, but we are going to take you in." He still had one hand on his gun.

A second county car pulled up, its lights flashing. A couple of surfing buddies drove by in the other lane waving and laughing. The second county cop got out of his car, also with his hand on his gun. As he approached, I saw that it was Bridgette's husband, Bob. He frowned and shook his head. He said a couple of words to Deputy Wilson and came over to my car with my license, insurance card, and registration.

"Duke, what's going on?" he asked.

I told him my side of the story—kind of. I didn't say I was tailing the phone company truck—I just said I was heading north to check out the surf up in Port Awful.

"And where's your surfboard? I can smell your wetsuit from here, but don't you need a board?" he asked, shooting a big hole in my story.

"Well, I thought I might do some body surfing," I countered. "Hmph," Bob said, scratching his chin. "I spoke with Wilson. We have to take you in."

"You're kidding me, right? I didn't do anything wrong. I just happened to be traveling in the same direction as that truck."

"Sorry, Duke. It's policy. Twice within twenty-four hours. C'mon, you can ride with me." By this time, Wilson had his gun out and was pointing it at me.

"Okay. Okay," I said. "Don't shoot. What about my car?"

"You've got twenty-four hours to move it or it will be impounded."

We arrived at the county jail a few minutes later. As luck would have it, Ursalik was there. "Hazzard? What are you doing here?"

"Well, Sarge, I thought I'd try out that latest fashions in handcuffs and orange jumpsuits," I joked. "Your big bad Deputy Wilson didn't like the way I was following his brother."

"Wilson! What are you up to now? I told you a couple days ago to leave that cat alone."

"But, Captain, he was following a truck too closely, and it's his second offense in twenty-four hours."

By this time Ursalik was fuming. "Did you *see* him follow too closely? Do we have anything worthwhile on him other than your brother's phone call?"

"Um. No, sir," Wilson said.

"Well then, as much as I'd like to lock him up until the day after I retire, release him," Ursalik said, shaking his head. "I'm not going to waste my time nor the judge's time on this." Turning to me, he said flatly, "Go. Get out of my sight, cat."

Bob released me from the handcuffs I had been wearing since I got out of my car. "My car! What about my car? Are you gonna give me a ride to my car?"

Ursalik look down at me. "No." He turned to Wilson and roughly grabbed him by the arm. "C'mon, Wilson, I gotta talk to you." The two of them disappeared behind a door into the jail. Deputy Joe Wilson is a big tough canine, but he's no match for the old grizzly. I could hear him howling at his deputy behind the closed door.

"Bob? Can you give me a ride?"

"Sorry, Duke," Bob said. "I can after my shift, but I'm doing a double and won't get off until midnight."

"That's bull crap, Bob, and you know it," I said.

"Sorry, Duke," Bob said again. "Even though we're not charging you, I still have an hour's worth of paperwork to do over this. I'm not real happy, either. C'mon, you can use the phone at my desk.

I called Trapper, and after a few minutes of whining and bribing, he reluctantly agreed to come get me. Once we got into his van, I told him about the phone company truck, the black boats, the seals, and the gill nets.

"Duke, you're gonna get yourself killed. Those seals are small, but they're ruthless. A cat's life doesn't hold much value with them," Trapper said.

"So maybe you can help me," I said. "Why don't you come with me tomorrow morning up to Limprock? We can take pictures of the black boats and the phone company truck."

"No thanks, Duke. A dog's life doesn't mean much to those seals, either. I'm not gonna get on their bad side."

Trapper dropped me off at my car. Before he drove away, he said, "Be careful, Duke. Maybe you should keep your nose out of that battle. You know that fable about a cat has nine lives is just that—a fable."

Needless to say, by this time I was not real happy, I was hungry, thirsty, and frustrated. It was a Friday afternoon—time to head to the bar for a large late lunch, then home to get to sleep to get up early. I wanted to be at Limprock before daylight. I drove over to the Stump and Grind, sat down, and watched Marge waddle toward my end of the bar. She deftly swooped up a cold glass and a bottle of Drab Light and after a pirouette reminiscent of the hippopotamuses in Disney's *Fantasia*, slid both in front of me.

"Wow, Marge. That was smooth," I said.

"I have moments," she replied with a grin. "I heard your name on the scanner a couple times today."

"Don't remind me. It's been a rough day," I muttered. "Can I get two of your slug-steak kabobs and an order of minced tuna lips?" I chugged my beer and said, "And another beer or two…or three. Thanks."

As I was finishing up beer number two and Marge was serving me my food, the front door slammed open and in walked four seals. I recognized two of them from Cary's, and I think the other two were on that large black boat. Yeah, they were part of the group that loaded the coolers into the phone company truck this morning, the truck that conveniently got away from me. They sat down at a table in the middle of the room talking loudly in that accent of theirs that's somewhere between Russian, Chinese, and Portuguese. One of them—one that was in the bait store—caught my eye. He stared at me for a little bit, turned to the others, and said something softly to them. They all turned to look at me, then turned back to talk with each other. Marge saw the whole thing and came over to me.

"You're okay, Duke. Those guys are pretty friendly. They've been coming in every afternoon for a couple weeks now. They're here from Canadia doing some fishing," she said, handing me beer number three.

I was getting an idea of just what kind of fishing they were doing. "Yeah, just the same, Marge, I think I'll drink up, pay up, and get outta here." I finished my beer and was pulling my wallet out of my back pocket as the front door opened again. In strode that odd Schnauzer that I saw up at the Poison Oak. She was wearing that weird uniform and was coming straight toward me.

"Are you Matthew?" she asked as she came up to me. "Your mother said I'd find you here."

The seals were watching this interaction and smirking. "Matthew," I heard one of them say.

"Yes. My name is Matthew, but call me Duke," I said. "Matthew. Duke," I heard from the seals' table.

"Well, Matthew, I have a job for you," the woman said. "Your mother said that you need a job."

"I have a job," I said. "Maybe my mother should keep her nose out of my business. Who are you and what kind of job?"

"I am Sergeant Helga Wigglebutt and a friend of your dear mother. She said that you are a private eye or something, right?"

"I am, and I'm on a case right now. Well, not *right* now. Right now I'm finishing my lunch and going to go take a nap."

"I want to hire you to be security at my store," she continued as if she hadn't heard a word I said. "It's a new resale shop with the proceeds going to the Shelter Valley Shelter for Wayward Puppies and Kittens. I will pay you $12 an hour. You start tonight, ten. South end of Dogstown. Can't miss it. Don't be late." With that, she nodded, turned on her heel, and started for the door.

"Hey, Wigglebutt! No! I'm not doing it," I yelled at her back as she went out the door. I turned back to Marge, who was trying hard not to laugh in my face. "How much do I owe you, Marge?"

I paid my tab, got in my car, and drove away. In the rearview mirror, I saw two of the seals standing outside the bar's door and watching me. *Well, Wigglebutt, the cat's out of the bag now*, I thought.

CHAPTER 11

Beware the Redhead!

Early the next morning, I drove up to Limprock. It was still dark, and I had a small flashlight that didn't want to stay on and a compact video camera that I picked up a couple years ago when I was tailing some guy whose wife was certain he was cheating on her. It turned out he was working a second job to pay the household bills because *she* was having an affair with someone and spending his money on gifts, hotels, and restaurants. Sometimes it's better not to even try and find these things out.

I parked my car behind a clump of willows and ducked into a thicket of scratchberry bushes. I was getting a little nicked and scraped up trying to get into position to video the boats when they came ashore. I was almost ready when my foot slipped out from under me on the dew-wetted leaves. My legs were cramping up, and I was just trying to move a little bit to get comfortable. I landed on my stomach, and my chin hit a rock. I slid face-first and facedown in the mud out from under the bush, down the bank, and onto the rock bar and right into the black shiny shoes of a uniformed DFW Ranger cat. (Shouldn't a Department of Fish & Wildlife officer be wearing some type of hiking boot? These looked more like city cop shoes.)

My camera (still stuck in the scratchberry bushes) was nowhere to be seen, and I wasn't going to mention it to the ranger. I also didn't mention my car.

The ranger was a big guy. He looked like Deputy Wilson but a little leaner. Could Wilson have another brother? A feline? He took me by the scruff of my neck and hauled me up into the front seat of his pickup truck. It was a big white official four-wheel four-door pickup with lights all over it.

"A little early in the morning to be berry-picking, wouldn't you say? I saw your flashlight in the bushes and had to check it out. Thanks for coming out without me having to go in after you." He started his truck and said, "I'm going to take you down to Crayfish Creek Campground. You'll be safe there. And there's lots of berries for you."

Crayfish Creek is a tributary to the Beaver Butt River about four miles from Limprock. There's a small (only eight spaces) campground there, which is hardly ever fully occupied. Probably because the sites are tiny, the bathroom is gross, there's no showers, and it's still a mile from the river's edge.

The ranger dropped me off there, switched on his flashing lights, and took off back towards Limprock. As I watched the truck leave, I could hear a jet boats motoring upstream. I started walking up the road back toward Limprock and my car. The sky to the east was starting to grow lighter, so I could see pretty well without the crappy flashlight that I purposely left in the ranger's pickup. The air was cool and crisp. There was a faint downstream breeze. The sound of the jet boat faded around the next bend in the river. Everything was quiet except for the crunch of my shoes on the gravel shoulder.

After hiking for barely five minutes, I could hear a car or a truck—some vehicle—coming down the road from the direction of Limprock—and right toward me. I could hear tires squealing as it maneuvered the winding river road. *I don't know what it is, but it's coming pretty fast*, I thought. In an instant, a pair of bright headlights shone around the curve in the road no more than fifty yards in front of me. I jumped into the ditch on the side of the road, which unfortunately had about four inches of slimy muck and rotted maple leaves in the bottom of it, instead of getting run over. As the vehicle went by, I saw that it was the same phone company truck that I've been chasing around, and right behind it was the DFW officer in his big white pickup truck on his tail but *without* his lights flashing. From my strategic vantage point, I could see them, but I don't think they saw me.

I crawled out of the ditch, wiped as much of the muck and leaves off me, and continued my hike up to Limprock. By the time I got there, the sun was fully up, and my car was still sitting behind the stand of willows. The army-surplus olive drab color helped conceal it. I pulled an old towel out from under a mostly dry wetsuit and cleaned myself up as good as I could. I went back to that copse of scratchberry bushes to look for my camera.

"Ah-ha! There you are." I reached into the thorny thicket and retrieved it. It was still on and in "record" mode, but the batteries had run down. I had the charger cord in my car, but nowhere to plug it in. I was halfway to Moleknuckle, so I decided to head up to John's house. I could plug it in there, and we could watch the playback with John and his otter brothers—maybe his sister, too.

I got to John's house, but it looked pretty empty. I knocked on the door anyway, waited a little while, and after no response, turned to leave. Just as I was stepping off the porch, I heard the door behind me open up. In the open doorway stood Willamina. She was wearing old sweats and a T-shirt. She looked like she just woke up. In the morning sunlight, she was gorgeous.

"I thought I heard somebody. Duke, what are *you* doing here?" she said. "And look at you, you're a mess. C'mon inside and take those clothes off."

I guess I was a little muddy from my swim in the ditch, and a little bloody from the scratchberries. I raised an eyebrow and looked sideways at her. "You want me to take my clothes off, hmmm?"

"Duke. Really?" She rolled her eyes and gave an exasperated sigh. "Yes. I'm going to throw your clothes in the washer while you take a shower. There's a towel in the bathroom, and you can wear Joe's bathrobe while your clothes are getting cleaned."

"Oh. I guess I'll have to live with disappointment again today." I smiled at her. "Oh wait. I gotta get something out of my car." I rushed out to Prince Valiant and grabbed my video camera and the charger cord. "We can charge this up while I'm in the shower."

I gave her a brief and very condensed version of this morning's events, telling her only that I was at Limprock doing some sur-veil-lance and that I think I had some evidence in my camera, but the batteries ran out. I omitted the part about the ranger, Crayfish Creek, and my dive into the ditch.

After I cleaned myself up and climbed into Joe's bathrobe, I followed the smell of coffee and frying bacon into the kitchen. It was still relatively early in the morning—only around eight—and a lot had already happened to me today *and on an empty stomach.*

"Something smells good in here!" I said as I walked into the kitchen. Willamina was standing at the sink doing dishes.

"Yup," she said. "Bacon and eggs. It was good. There's still some coffee if you want some."

"Oh," I said, a little confused. "Did you already eat?"

"Well, yeah. I made myself breakfast while you were in the shower. I just got up when you got here. I had customers in the bar until late last night so I slept in."

"Hmm," was all I could say while my stomach growled in protest. "Um, sure. Coffee sounds great."

"Cups are in the cupboard, and the coffeepot's on the counter." With that, she walked out of the kitchen, saying over her shoulder, "Your clothes should be ready for the dryer."

I got a coffee mug, filled it with dark brown steaming hot coffee, and sat down at the kitchen table. *More disappointment*, I thought to myself. By then my video camera was charged enough to turn on, but I kept it plugged in. I flipped open the small video screen on the side of the camera and pushed the "playback" button.

"You clothes will be done in about twenty minutes," Willamina said as she came back into the kitchen. "So what's on your little TV?"

"When I lost my footing and fell out from under the scratch-berries, I dropped the camera."

"Wait. What? You fell out from 'under the scratchberries'?"

"Yeah. Anyway, my camera landed in the bushes and kept filming. I…um…ran into a DFW Ranger, and he suggested that I vacate the area for a little while. I told him I was picking berries, and he gave me a ride to Crayfish Creek, where the berry picking was better."

"Wait. You're not telling me the whole story," she said. "What did this ranger look like? Tall? Feline? Broad shoulders? Drives a big white truck?"

"Yeah. That's him. So anyway," I continued, "my camera kept filming while—"

She interrupted, "I know that guy. He was at the bar late last night. He was drinking and shooting pool with those seals that chased you out the other day."

This conversation was not going well. To her, I kept looking more and more like a fool with every passing second. "They didn't 'chase me out.' I just thought that there was nothing more I could learn there and I left."

"You didn't finish your beer or pay your tab. Sure looked like you turned tail and ran," she said, smirking.

"No. Okay. Anyway back to the camera—"

"No. Wait. So this ranger—his name is Felix, by the way—takes you down to Crayfish Creek? What about your car? How'd you get back to Limprock?"

Embarrassingly, I told her—in detail because she kept asking me pesky little questions—the whole series of events from the time I fell into Ranger Felix until I arrived at her doorstep.

"Well, Duke, all I can say is you do not lead a boring life." She laughed when I finished my tale. "Let's see what's on your camera."

The camera had hung up in the thorns and branches so it wasn't lined up as perfectly as I had wished. The angle was off by about forty-five degrees, so you had to twist your neck to see it, and it only caught—just barely—the very last foot or so of the truck, but it did capture the seals arriving and loading large black coolers into the truck.

"Perfect!" I said. "Now I've got evidence. I'm gonna turn this over to Ursalik, and he can take it from here."

The buzzer from the dryer announced that my laundry was finished. Willamina stood and said over shoulder as she walked out of the room, "No, you're not!"

"It's the seals! They're poaching the salmon. I'll bet Scottie was killed by the seals because he caught them doing it!"

She came back in with my shirt, pants, socks, and skivvies, which she put in a pile on the kitchen table. "Duke, you have no proof. All you have is a grainy, out-of-focus, short video clip of some seals load-ing something into a truck. You have no proof of them doing any-thing wrong, what's in the coolers, or who any of them are."

"Yeah, maybe you're right. Ursalik would laugh at me and probably keep my camera. Nothing would get done. It would be 'case closed,' and the seals would keep on doing what they're doing, and somebody else at some time will suffer."

"Is there anyone in the sheriff's office that you trust?" she asked. "Maybe you could talk with them."

"There is one guy. I know his wife. They're both real nice. But same thing. I need more evidence. I'm going to head back to town and check some stuff out. Plus it's Saturday. The county's closed."

"Do you want any help?" she asked.

"Nah, I don't know what or where I'm gonna do or go."

"I thought maybe you'd take me to lunch or something. I *did* wash your clothes, you know." She smiled a broad beaming white smile. She looked gorgeous.

"Yes! Thank you for that. Really. How about we meet later for dinner?"

"Okay," she said. "It's a date. I haven't been to Swindler's in a while. This will be fun!"

Swindler's Chop House was the most expensive restaurant on either side of the Butt. It was pricey, but it was good, and if Willamina wanted to have a date with me there, I was more than happy with that!

"Cool," I said. "Five o'clock?"

"Sure."

"I'll make reservations." I stood and grabbed my pile of clothes—still warm from the dryer—and changed into them in the bathroom. When I came out and went back to the kitchen, my video camera was on the table along with a little note that read, "Had to run. See you tonight. Please lock the door behind you." I looked up and saw a small rusty pickup truck pull out of the driveway, kicking up a cloud of dust as it left.

Hmmm. That is one strange woman, I thought. *I better get out of here. Maybe this 'date' could turn into something tonight. I better clean up my place.*

I drove down the river road into town, thinking things through in my mind and saying out loud, "There has always been bad blood between the otters and the seals, but they rarely escalated to murder and never over fish. The ranger has something to do with this, so does that phone company truck. And it was about this time yesterday that the phone truck was at the port!" I stepped on the accelerator pedal, and after thinking about it for a little, Prince Valiant decided to actu-ally accelerate. I love my car, but he can be a little slow to react.

As quickly as I could, I drove into town and down to the port area. I parked at the side of the post office in the shadow of the building where I had a direct line of sight to the marina. Just as I arrived, the crew from the large black boat were carrying two large coolers up the dock. The phone company truck was backing down the boat ramp toward them. I pulled out my video camera, slunk down in my seat, and using the screen on the side as the viewfinder, filmed the loading operation from the post office parking lot. In less than a couple minutes, the coolers were in the truck, the seals were heading back to their boat, and the truck was driving up the ramp. The truck turned toward me. I kept the camera recording as I slid further down in the seat so as not to be seen. As the truck drove past me, I aimed the camera at the driver, and he looked right at it—a full face shot. I saw him pick up his cell phone and start dialing.

"Oh crap!" I said aloud. "He's calling his brother for sure." I kept filming the truck as it drove away and was able to zoom in and focus on the license plate, but quickly turned the machine off, started up my car, and headed in the opposite direction. I drove through the marina and turned onto Airport Road. Airport Road runs between the one-strip Dogstown airport and the beach. The road was basically built on the sand dunes, so it's full of dips, potholes, heaves, and cracks. It's impossible to go very fast without bouncing off into the sand on either side of the road, but I figured that Wilson would come from the other direction and he'd have to drive this road as well. Airport Road ends and becomes 4th street, which goes right past McRay's Market. I pulled into the grocery store parking lot, put my camera in the trunk, and hurried into the store. I was looking over my shoulder as I entered the store. Deputy Wilson pulled in, and since I wasn't watching where I was going, I ran smack into someone coming out with both arms full of groceries. Both of her bags fell and spilled open on the store's floor. I bent to help pick up and rebag the cans, bottles, bananas, oranges. I saw a pair of sensible brown shoes and beige knee socks. Looking up I saw the face of Sergeant Helga Wigglebutt looking down at me. And she didn't look too happy.

"Matthew Hazzard," she said sternly. "I am very disappointed in you. You didn't show up to work yesterday. That is not good, but I am a fair person. I will give you one more chance."

"Listen, Wigglebutt," I said, handing her, her two bags of gro-ceries. "I don't work for you. I don't *want* to work for you. Find someone else." I looked over her shoulder and saw Bridgette Maypox pushing a cart with a baby in the seat and another child tagging along behind. "As a matter of fact, lady, I am working on a case right now, and you might have put me in danger yesterday at the Stump. At the very least, you tipped my hand to some people in the bar."

Bridgette disappeared down aisle four. I turned and looking through the large plate glass windows of the storefront window saw Deputy Wilson pull his county sheriff 's car into the parking space next to mine. Wigglebutt followed my glance, saw the deputy get out of the car, and turned to look at me again. Her lips were pursed tightly together. She raised her finger and pointed it right into my face.

"I knew it. I should have believed your mother," she said. "You're in some sort of trouble, aren't you?"

"I don't have time for this, lady. I gotta go." I pushed past her, knocking one of her bags of groceries out of her hands. This time, the bag broke when it hit the floor, and so did a bottle of ammonia. I caught up with Bridgette and her two kittens in the frozen foods aisle. She was loading a half dozen frozen pizzas into her cart.

They were the cheap cheese, thin weak sauce, and toad sausage ones. To me, those pizzas taste more like cardboard and ketchup than pizza. The packaging would be more flavorful.

"Hi, Bridgette," I said. "Imagine running into you here."

"From what I saw a few minutes ago, you're pretty good at running into people here," she said with a smirk.

"Oh that. Yeah, she's a friend of my mom's. She wants me to work for her."

"Mmm-hmm. Sure."

"So who are these two?" I asked, tousling the curly red hair of the little one standing next to his mom's cart's. The little boy got an immediate snarl on his face, and he reached up and punched me right in the most sensitive area of a male body. As I doubled over in pain, the little girl in the cart's seat started bawling at the top of her lungs.

"Thanks, Duke," Bridgette said as she lifted the little girl out of the cart. "There, there. You're okay. Shhhh. It's okay. Bobby didn't mean it."

"I did too," the little boy shot back. "I don't like strangers touching my hair."

The little girl quieted down, and Bridgette put her back in the seat. "Now, Bobby, apologize to Mr. Hazzard."

"No. He should apologize to *me*," the boy said, folding his arms and turning his back on his mom.

"Sorry, Duke," Bridgette said. "People warned me about a red-head's temper. I thought he'd grown out of once he passed the terrible twos, but apparently not. Are you okay?"

"I'm fine," I squeaked. My voice was temporarily—I hoped—a couple octaves higher. "But I *am* glad I saw you here. Is there any way I could get in touch with your husband? I want to talk with him about Deputy Wilson."

"Are you in trouble?" she asked. She was looking over my shoulder and out into the parking lot. "It looks like Joe is interested in your car."

I turned and saw Deputy Wilson looking through the driver's side window of my car. *Good thing I put the camera in the trunk. That's gotta be what he's looking for*, I thought. "I think he's interested in what's in it," I replied.

"But, yeah, we can call Bob right now, he's at the park playing batball with the twins." She pulled a cell phone out of her purse. It was one of those new *smartphones*. I think they're called that because they make people like me look stupid. As she started dialing, she lowered her voice to almost a whisper, she said, "I don't like that guy, and if you two can get him out of the county offices, my life would be *so much* better."

"Hello? Bob?" she spoke into the phone. "Hey, I'm at the store, and Duke is here. He wants to talk with you." She handed me the phone.

I'm still not too familiar with cell phones, especially the smart ones. They're a relatively new technology for me, and this is such a rugged and remote area that most people that I know that have them say that they only work in certain places. My secretary, Cathie, has one, but she doesn't even get reception in my office. She has to stand out on the doorstep on one foot with her other arm in the air to use the thing. So of course, when Bridgette handed me the phone, I pressed the disconnect button and hung up on Bob. But I didn't know that and thought he was on the other end. "Hello? Hello? Bob?" I spoke at the device.

It started humming and vibrating, and panicking, I handed it back to Bridgette.

"Hello?" Bridgette said into the phone. "Oh. Hi, honey. Yes he's right here. No, I don't know why he hung up on you. Here he is." She gave me the phone again.

Gingerly, I put the phone to my ear. "Bob? Oh great. It works. Yeah Hi, how ya' doin'? Hey, I was wondering if we could get together and discuss some stuff about a case I'm working on. Today? Yeah, that'd be great. Five o'clock? Sure. How about I buy you a beer at the Stump and Grind? Cool. Thanks. See you there."

I handed Bridgette the phone again. She spoke into it, "Remember the birthday party tonight. Bobby will be pretty upset if you're not there. Right. Six o'clock at the Ernst's. Okay. See you soon. Love you, too."

She hung up the phone, put it back into her purse, and turned to me.

"Don't keep him too long, please. Today is one of his only days off, and we have a three-year-old's birthday party to go to." She pointed at the cart, which also had five gallons of ice cream in addition to the half dozen pizzas. "As you can see, I'm bringing food."

"No problem, Bridgette, we'll be done by 5:45. Or earlier. I really appreciate this. Thank you," I said.

I looked out at the parking lot again. Wigglebutt was storming up to Deputy Wilson. She turned and pointed at the store. I could easily read her lips as she said, "He's in there."

Wilson started walking toward the store.

"Hey, Bridgette," I said. "Don't look now, but here comes our buddy."

Wilson was walking toward us, coming down the frozen foods aisle, glaring at me. He saw Bridgette, recognized her, and gave a small halfway smile. I turned to walk the other way.

"Hold it right there, Hazzard," he said loudly and with authority. "I need to talk with you."

I froze in my tracks and slowly turned toward him. Bridgette turned her cart and momentarily blocked his path. "Hello, Mrs. Maypox. Good to see you out of the office. And who's this little guy?" He reached down and tousled Bobby's hair. Bobby got that same look on his face, and next thing I knew, Wilson was bent over in pain, the little girl was crying loudly, and I was making cat tracks in the opposite direction.

"Ooof! Get back here, Hazzard!" the big canine gasped. Bobby got him good. Minutes later, I was back in my car and heading back to the feline side of the Butt.

Whew. That was close, I thought. *I wonder who taught that kid that trick? He sure has good aim*!

I drove back to my little apartment, retrieved my camera from the trunk, went inside, and flopped down on the couch. I flipped open the screen and hit the "playback" button.

"Bingo!" I said aloud. "Take *that*, Willamina! *Now* I've got proof! Oh crap! Willamina!"

I picked up the phone and dialed the number Willamina had given me. A male voice answered.

"Um hello," I said. "Uh. This is Duke Hazzard. Is Willamina there?"

"Oh. Hello, Mr. Duke. This is Joe, her brother," said the voice. "She not here. She at work."

"Hi, Joe. So she's at the Poison Oak?"

"Yes. You call her there. Bye." He hung up.

I looked up the number in the phone book and dialed the Poison Oak. This time a female voice answered and in a bored monotone, as if she had repeated the same thing five thousand times already that day, said, "Hello, thank you for calling the Poison Oak Cafe and Lounge, home of the humongous burger. This is Willamina. How may I brighten your day?"

"By coming to dinner with me tonight at Swindler's," I replied, trying to mimic the same bored tone.

"Duke! Hi, honey!" she said in a much happier voice. "Honey? Really?" I said surprised.

"Oh, I call everyone that. What's up?"

"Well, there's been a slight change in plans."

"Oh, now what?" she asked, clearly disappointed.

"No, no, really. It's good," I said quickly. "We're going to the Stump and Grind at five o'clock and—"

"What? The Stump, not Swindler's? That's not *good*, Duke. That's bad."

"No, you didn't let me finish," I said, still trying to sound cheerful. "We're meeting a friend there who's a sheriff's deputy to show him the video."

"What? Duke, I thought we talked about that this morning," she scolded. "First, you have no proof. Second, I don't trust the cops."

"Well, first, I now *do* have proof. I have the face of the driver of the phone company truck and the license plate number of the truck on my video camera. And second, I trust this guy. I know his wife, and he's a good man. His wife works for the county as well, and neither of them like nor trust Wilson. He's on our side."

"Hmmm…" was all she said. I could tell this wasn't the evening that she had in mind.

"I promised his wife that we'd be done by 5:45. After that, we go to Swindler's. I have reservations for 6:00," I lied.

"Hmmm…" she said again. "We'll see. Madge's at 5:00? Maybe you'll see me. Maybe you won't." She hung up.

CHAPTER 12

Seems a Little Thin

Saturday night

Ipulled into The Stump and Grind parking lot at 5:01. Pretty good for me. I'd say I was almost early. As I was getting my video camera out of the trunk of my car, Bob drove up and parked next to me. We felines share the same ideas about punctuality. Willamina was already there. I saw her truck in the parking lot.

"Hi, Bob," I said, closing my trunk and extending a hand to him. "Hello, Duke. Whatcha got there?" he asked, nodding toward the camera in my hand.

I stashed the camera inside my open jacket. It was a very valuable commodity, and I didn't know who was in the bar. "I'll show you. C'mon, let's get a beer. There's also someone here I would like you to meet. She's a little distrustful of 'the authorities,'" I said, doing those silly air quotes. "Maybe you can change her mind."

Bob and I walked in together. At the bar were Tater and Fang. Behind the bar was Marge, of course. Butch and Ginger were also there, sitting at a table in the middle of the room. At another table were the four seals that were there the day before. I looked closely at them—as closely as I could without them noticing that I was. I didn't really recognize them from the video, but it was possible that one or two of them were on that black boat. Willamina was sitting at a small table in the corner. As we walked toward her, I heard the word *Duke* coming from the direction of the seals. I turned to see if someone was calling to me, but the seals were huddled over their beers and not looking at me. Bob and I sat down at Willamina's table. I introduced the two of them to each other. I started to pull out my camera to show Bob and Willamina the latest footage, but hesitated. Ginger's voice was rising rapidly.

"…there were four hundred cats there and we weren't invited!"

"I know, dear. Apparently, I guess, there wasn't enough room for us," Butch said, trying to calm her down.

"She's your mother!" Ginger shouted, spit-spraying her mai tai across Butch's face. "It was her seventieth birthday, and '*there wasn't room?* Hmmmph!" She sat down and stiffly folded her arms across her chest. She turned away from Butch in drunken disgust and then caught sight of me as I tried to hide behind Willamina.

"Hey! Duke!" she said, getting up and smiling. "Butchie, look! It's Duke!" She started coming over toward our table. Butch reached across their table and attempted to grab her arm and sit her back down. "Let go of me," she said to Butch, yanking her arm from his grasp. Turning around and striding, well more like staggering in my direction, she said to me, "Your buddy Trapper owes me a new camera. He threw me into the river!"

"No, Ginger. Honest, he didn't mean anything. He just barely touched you and—"

Before I could finish my sentence, she slurred, "Yesh, I know. Dogs will be dogs, right? Ha!"

By this time, Butch was on his feet and coming toward our table, too. "Okay, Ginger, let's go home okay?"

Ginger fell backward into Butch's arms. "Nice catch," the cop said. "You gotta get her outta here, Butch, before she hurts herself."

"I know. Right. Here we go, honey," Butch said, pulling Ginger toward the exit.

Right then, Ginger caught her balance and stood up, shaking off Butch's grip. "I'm okay. I'm okay. Lemme go," she spat out. She turned to Butch and said, "I love you, honey. Take me home." She melted into his arms.

"Yes, dear," said Butch, uttering the safest two words of every husband's vocabulary.

But Ginger wasn't quite through. She bolted upright and spun around. She pointed at me and said, "You know, Duke, Faye is an *awesome* girl. Yeah! You two should get married!" She turned and fell into Butch again. "Don't you think they'd have adorable kittens, Butchie?" And with that last bit of energy expended, her head fell into Butch's chest. I thought I could already hear her snoring.

Butch looked over her at me and silently mouthed, "Sorry, Duke." He half-led, half-dragged his inebriated wife out of the back exit. The screen door slammed behind them.

"Who's Faye?" Willamina asked with a sideways grin. "Kittens?" I rolled my eyes and said, "She's this gal who works for the newspaper, and Ginger is trying hard to get us together. She's nice, I suppose, but I don't really have any feelings for her. Okay?"

"Really?" she asked, teasing me.

"Really," I said firmly. "Now can we get to business?"

"Right," Bob said. "Bridgette gave me a message to pass along that she thinks might find interesting. Apparently Judy Boodles's father, Aris, bought a big chunk of land up at the north end of the county, New Flowers Lake, right when she was hired."

"Yeah, and?" I asked.

"Well, it turns out that the property taxes he paid are almost the exact same amount of funds needed to cover Joe Wilson's salary and benefit package. She thinks it just might be a coincidence, but that it might be something, seeing as Wilson was hired with the implied intent of keeping an eye on old man Boodles's only daughter."

"It might be something."

"What caught Bridgette's eye was that he paid three years' worth of taxes to get to that amount—one year of back taxes, one year of current taxes, and another year's in advance. She says that that is not uncommon and some banks require you to do so when purchasing a foreclosure—which this was."

"All right. Something else to wonder about," I said. "How is Boodles to work for?"

"Don't really know. I don't have much interaction with city administration, but she seems nice. Quiet, but nice," Bob replied. "Okay, now whatcha got, Duke? I don't have much time."

I gave Bob a review of my theory that Felix the ranger and the Wilson brothers are working for the herd of seals, illegally poaching salmon both in the river and the near shore, and when Scottie found out what they were up to, he got killed.

"I think it could be the seals are working for them," Willamina said. "It sure looked like Felix was the boss last night. He paid the tab and looked like he was giving orders not getting them."

"Hmmmm…" I said. "Yeah. You could be right. I don't know. I still haven't figured out who actually killed Scottie, either."

"My brothers are pretty sure it was the seals, but there's no proof. And that's what I was talking about this morning. Proof. Remember, Duke?"

"Let's see what's on your camera," Bob said.

I opened up the side screen and hit the "playback" button. After the first recording where my camera was stuck in the bushes, I showed them the latest footage from the marina. "See? I caught them loading the illegal fish into the truck, I got the driver's face, and I got the license plate," I said proudly.

"Again, Duke. That's not proof of anything except some seals loading some coolers into a truck," Willamina said.

"Actually, there's enough here to open an investigation," Bob chimed in. "But until we know more about who at the county is in on it, we have to keep it quiet. Is it just Joe Wilson, or are there others?"

"Seems a little thin," Willamina said. "So okay. What's next then?"

"Here's what I think our next steps should be," I said. "Bob, can you run those plates and see who owns the truck? It certainly isn't the phone company."

"I already wrote down the numbers. I will trace it from my patrol car tomorrow."

"Great. Now, Willamina, the Wilsons don't know who you are, so can you follow the truck after it leaves the marina tomorrow?"

"What? Me?" she asked.

"Yeah, you're the only one. Bob can't. I can't," I said. "Just stay way behind them, and when they pull into where they're going, you keep going. If we can find out what they're doing with the fish, we might have a better idea of who is working for who," I said.

"That's kind of what I was thinking," said Bob. "I think there might be someone else behind this that hired both the seals and the Wilsons."

"So I'm gonna tail the truck, Bob's going to find out more about the truck and who might be helping at the county. What are *you* gonna do, Duke?" Willamina asked.

"I'm going to go fishing and see if I can't get some footage of the seals pulling nets."

"I don't think that's a good idea, Duke," Bob said. "You go it alone and you'll end up like Scottie. How about this? We'll get some folks together, a couple boats. Safety in numbers. I've got a friend that I trust, and he's a river patrolman for the Forest Circus. I'll call him tomorrow."

"My brothers can take you out. I'm sure they'd want to help," Willamina added.

"The more, the better. I'll take my boat, too," I said.

"*You* have a boat?" Willamina asked, almost sounding a little impressed.

"Well, technically it belongs to Butch, but I can use it any time. It's at my house. I named it the *Steelhead Slayer* or just *Slayer*.

"It's a *new* boat?" Willamina asked, sounding even more impressed. "Well, no. New to me, at least," I said, trying to sound impressive. Willamina's eyes narrowed. She was squinting at me like her big brother, giving me the look like she's not believing any of my story.

"What was the boat's name when you got it?"

"*Myrtle*," I replied sheepishly.

"Oh, you have the *Myrtle*? That's a cool old boat," she said. "I thought it was gone. I thought it was made into a flower bed or was on someone's trash heap or something. Don't you dare rename her. She's a classic."

"It's bad luck—" Bob started.

I cut him off with, "I know, I know. It's bad luck to rename a boat. Everybody has already told me."

"Okay then. Listen. I gotta run," Bob said, standing. "Let's touch base tomorrow afternoon. Maybe we can pull this off on Monday. I've got a birthday party to get to, and my three-year-old won't be happy if I'm late."

"And that's one kid you don't wanna piss off!" I added.

Bob laughed. "Right, Bridgette told me about that. At least he got Wilson. And I think he got him pretty good, too."

Willamina looked sideways at both of us. Bob left as I gave her a recap of the little redheaded devil with a wicked right hook. "So dinner at Swindler's?" I asked.

"Nah. I'm gonna head home. Raincheck?"

"Really? Okay, sure. A raincheck." This woman was nothing if not pure disappointment.

CHAPTER 13

Shear Bad luck

Sunday

I called Trapper the next morning to see if he wanted to go fish-ing upriver with me on Monday.

"Well, I don't know, Duke," Trapper said. "Are they catching anything up there? I had heard that the fish were all down in the bay waiting for the first rains to come. I don't wanna go if we don't have much of a chance to catch anything."

"I went out on Thursday with my clients—they're otters—and we caught a couple steelhead."

"They don't count. Otters and seals can always find fish. It's in their genes," he replied.

"That's a little racist, isn't it?"

"It would be if it wasn't true."

"Okay, here's the real reason…" I explained to him what Bob, Willamina, and I had come up with the night before. "We're just going to take some pictures. Maybe we'll catch a fish or two. We'll have otters with us."

"No, Duke. I think I'm gonna sit this one out. If you want to troll around in the bay, I could probably come with you, but I don't want to get between any seal or otter," he said.

"Well, I guess I'll have one of Willamina's brothers in my boat tomorrow."

"Lemme know how it goes." Trapper hung up.

I drove into town and went to Cary's Tackle Box. Cary was there smoking one of his short, sweet cigars.

"Hey, Duke," he said. "What are you up to today?"

"Not sure, Cary," I replied. Half-jokingly, I asked, "Where are the fish biting today?"

"Still jammed up in the bay."

"Hmmm…that's what Trapper said, too."

"Yeah, the fall salmon run is waiting for rains to flush down the river. The rain will lower the water temperature, which allows it to have more dissolved oxygen, making it easier for them to breathe. Also, as the rivers rise a little bit and the small tributary streams fill with water, grasses, leaves, twigs, and other debris are swept downstream, which the fish can smell, and it triggers something in their brain that says it's time to get moving toward their spawning grounds."

"What about the steelhead I caught last Thursday?" I asked. "Where were you fishing?"

"I was with John and two of his brothers, and we launched from Limprock and went upstream from there. Not too far, maybe a mile or so," I replied.

"Oh, okay. Right. Those were summer steelhead. Summer steelhead—as well as the spring salmon run—are immature fish. They enter the river immature and mature on their way to their spawning ground. Generally, these are fish that have a long way to travel, maybe 250 miles or so, and they take a few months to do so."

"Now I'm confused. Isn't a steelhead a salmon?" I asked.

"No. A steelhead is actually an ocean-going rainbow trout. And actually I heard the summer steelhead are biting—and people are catching 'em up by Limprock. If you don't wanna circle around in the bay, you could try that up there."

"Really? Maybe I'll hook up the *Slayer* and try my luck," I said.

"*Slayer*? Did you get a new boat? I thought Butch gave you the ol' *Myrtle*."

"Well, yeah, he did, but I call her the *Steelhead Slayer*. I didn't *rename* her. That's just what I call her."

Jim took a draw off his cigar and said, "Good 'cause it's bad luck—"

I cut him off, "I know, I know. It's bad luck to rename a boat. I know."

"Okay, well. Do you have steelhead gear?"

"What do you mean?" I asked.

"Duke, you need entirely different gear for steelhead than salmon."

"Hmmm…" I could feel my wallet getting lighter already. "Okay, set me up, I guess."

He sold me a different rod and reel combo—a more sensitive rod, thinner lighter line, and a spinning reel—along with more steelhead-specific spinners and lures. It cost me a couple hundred dollars, but it was pretty cool stuff. Definitely more delicate than the stout salmon tackle I had. The line was a braided monofilament that was so thin and light I couldn't wait to cast with it. The rod was really "whippy" and flexible. The reel was a golden color and was light. The spinners and lures were shiny silver and pink. Cary said that steelhead like pink while salmon go for green. Who was I to argue?

I went home, hooked the trailer to the car, and drove up to Limprock. Before I put the boat in the water, I thought I'd try a few practice casts with my new outfit. I wasn't expecting to catch anything, I just wanted to give it a test run before I had to split my concentration between operating the boat and the rod and reel. I walked down to the river's edge and cast my lure out into the water. It floated out over the mirrored surface and landed with an almost silent hint of a splash.

Just beautiful, I thought.

I was standing almost knee-deep in clear cool water. The alder and maple trees along the banks were just beginning to show their autumn colors, and a few red, orange, green, and yellow leaves drifted by in the lazy current. It was late morning, and the river's canyon walls were so steep that the sun had yet to hit the water, but was lighting up the foliage closer to the ridgelines on both sides. Everything was still. I heard a loud "squaaarrrkk" and, looking up, saw a large great blue heron slowly winging his way downstream along the other bank. There wasn't a cloud in the deep blue sky. All was quiet. I could easily imagine that I could be the first human to stand in that spot.

This sure beats trolling around in a circle in the windy bay, breathing outboard-motor exhaust fumes with a bunch of other people.

I really didn't care if I caught anything at all, just being right there, right then was satisfaction. I started reeling in and immedi-ately my rod-tip started shaking like a Chihuahua standing on an iceberg. I pulled back slightly and set the hook—or so I thought. A sliver of silver exploded from the water about twenty yards away from where I was standing. I swear the fish looked at me, winked, and casually spit out my fancy pink lure. There's an old fishing adage that proclaims, "Nothing in nature grows as fast as the fish that just got away." Within minutes—in my mind—that little eight-inch trout had grown into a full-sized twelve-pound steelhead.

I casted out a few more times, but not a nibble. I imagined that the fish who took my lure had gone back to his—or her—little silver friends and they were getting a good laugh out of me by now. I got back into Prince Valiant and backed the boat down the ramp and into the water. I tied her off to the small floating dock, parked my car and trailer out of the way, and went back down to *Myrtle*, dba *Steelhead Slayer*. I motored out into the calm water and quickly noticed that the current upriver was considerably stronger than down in the estuary of the Butt. I gave the little engine some more gas, and we started making headway upstream. I wanted to go to the same spot that I went to with John and his brothers. We caught fish up there. I pushed the throttle a little more and was soon throwing out a decent-sized bow wake as I plowed against the current. I was loving it. The wind was a little chilly in my face and was making my eyes tear. It was beautiful, and I was in feline heaven.

The next thing I knew—or didn't know—the boat came to an abrupt stop. I was thrown up against the steering wheel and jammed against the windshield. The motor was whining loudly, and slowly the boat started drifting back downstream. Shaking off the cobwebs in my brain, I throttled the motor back down and looked around to try and figure out what happened. Apparently my little boat doesn't go as well in the shallow parts of the river as John's flat-bottomed jetboat, and I had run aground in water that was no more than eight inches deep. And now something was wrong with the engine. It was running, but I wasn't moving. I tried putting it in reverse and no luck. Forward? Nothing. I turned the motor off and wishing I had remembered to buy an actual oar with my new fishing gear, pulled out the old water ski and started paddling. Fortunately, the current was taking me right toward Limprock.

I drifted back downriver toward the campground and using the ski, was able to land on the rocky shore about fifty yards downstream from the boat ramp.

Well, I guess that takes my boat out of the lineup for tomorrow's operation, I thought as I was walking up to get my car and trailer. I backed the trailer down the ramp and went and got my boat. Using a short section of rope I found in my trunk, I started pulling my boat along the shore toward my car. I was almost waist-deep and struggling to drag the *Slayer* up the bank, over the shallows, and against the current when another boat with a couple feline fishermen in it arrived from downriver.

"Y'all need a tow?" the driver of the boat yelled as they approached. "That'd be great!" I shouted back.

"Ya know, it'd probably be easier if you lifted your motor up. It's dragging on the rocks," the other guy in the boat said. The driver pulled his boat up alongside my boat, and the passenger climbed aboard, reached around behind the engine, flipped a lever, and tilted the motor forward, raising the propeller out of the water.

I was still standing in the water holding on to the rope tied to the bow. She seemed lighter all of a sudden. "Wow. Thanks!" I said. "Didja run outta gas?" the driver asked, reaching a hand out to me. "Here, gimme that bow line."

"No. It just stopped working. The engine runs, but it doesn't go in forward or reverse," I said, letting him take the rope and hand it to his buddy, who tied it to a cleat at the stern of his boat.

I waded to shore and then trotted back to the boat ramp where my car was waiting. The two boats arrived a minute later. The pas-senger threw the rope to me, and I pulled the boat in, floated it onto the trailer, and hooked up the winch line. I cranked the boat up snug to the winch, got in my car, and drove up the ramp.

The driver of the other boat tied off to the small dock and started walking up the ramp. As I was tying my boat down to the trailer, he came up, looked at my propeller, and shook his head. "Oh man!" he said. "This prop's pretty frickin' beat up. Didja run aground or sump'n?"

"Yeah," I said sheepishly. "I guess I can't get too shallow with her."

"An' you said thet the engine runs but the prop don't wanna turn?"

"Yeah," I said, really feeling like a fool.

"Well, you prolly sheared the pin."

"I what?"

He explained to me the concept of the shear pin. "There's a small round metal pin that fits through a hole in the driveshaft that holds the propeller in place. It's designed to break when you hit something, like you did, instead of the driveshaft breaking." We looked in the glove box of the boat and found a small box with spare pins. He replaced the broken pin with a new one. "An' thar ya go," he said after he had reassembled everything. "An' ja know, if you tilt yer motor up when ya launch it, ya won't hafta back down so far."

"Thanks," I said. "Really, thanks for everything." I climbed back into Prince Valiant and after a quick lunch of deep-fried mole clusters and rutabaga rootball salad at the Stump, I went home.

There were two messages on my answering machine—the first was from Bob.

"Hey, Duke, it's Bob. My Forest Circus friend—Steve DiChincho—is fully on board with helping us tomorrow morning. We need to meet at Crayfish Creek at 5:00 a.m., latest. We're going to use his patrol boat. We need to be on the water and up to Limprock before first light at 6:00 a.m.," the message said.

The second call was from Willamina. "Duke! Duke! It's Willamina!" she quickly said in an excited whisper. "Ha-ha, I feel like Mata Hari! Anyway, I followed the truck to Port Awful. It pulled into one of those refrigerated warehouses down on the docks. It got there just as a large overhead door was opening up. It closed right behind it. I'm pretty confident nobody saw me. When the truck turned into the warehouse, I came over here to Redtide Fish 'n Chips and am having lunch. I can see the warehouse from here. Wait! Wait! There's three guys walking out! One of them is definitely Felix, the ranger. One of them is the driver, but I can't tell which one—they look like twins. Wow! This is exciting! They're getting into a silver SUV. They're driving back towards CatsCamp!" she whispered. "Okay. I'm gonna finish my lunch and head home. Give me a call."

Hmmm… I thought. *So that confirms that the three of them are connected to the salmon poaching, but we still don't have a suspect for the murder of Scottie the otter.*

I picked up the phone and dialed. John answered, "Hullo?"

"Um, yeah, hi. This is Duke. Is Willamina there?"

"Ah, Mr. Duke! This is John. We go with you tomorrow. We catch Scottie's killer. Here is Willamina."

"Duke?" a female voice said. "I already told him about tomorrow's operation. I told him that we are meeting at Limprock at 5:30."

"No. We're meeting at Crayfish at 5:00. We don't want them to see our cars, especially Steve's Forest Circus patrol car. We'll motor up to Limprock from there."

"This is so exciting, Duke. Thank you," she said. "I will make it up to you. See you tomorrow, honey." She hung up.

CHAPTER 14

Let's Go Fishing!

It was 4:30, Monday morning. Well, the clock said it was morning. As far as I was concerned, it was the middle of the night. I had called out and had an anchovy and Gorgonzola pizza delivered the night before and washed it down with a six-pack I picked up down at Nasim's. I had had the *Slayer* hitched up to my car and didn't feel like dealing with unhitching it last night just to hook it back up in the morning. I made a cup of coffee, poured it into a used paper cup that I fished out of the trash, and drove up to Crayfish Creek Campground. I got there at 4:45.

John, Willamina, and their brothers weren't there yet, but Bob and Steve were. They were backing their boat down the ramp. I immediately had boat envy. The Forest Circus patrol boat was long and sleek and clean. The instrument panel looked like what I imagine an airline jet's cockpit would look like. There were two radios, lots of dials and gauges and switches. They effortlessly floated the boat off the trailer and tied it up to the dock.

"Good morning, Duke," Bob said. "C'mere, I want you to meet Steve."

"Nice boat," I said as Steve walked up the ramp towards us.

"Yeah, thanks. It gets around," he said, smiling. He was a feline in full uniform. Actually both Bob and Steve were wearing their uniforms, including badges and guns. He was about my height, maybe an inch taller, but he probably outweighed my scrawny frame by twenty-five pounds—none of it fat. He had icy blue eyes and a firm, strong handshake. "Nice to meet you, Duke. Bob has told me about the work you've done on this case. Thank you," he said.

"I was working on this same case for a while until the state took it over, claiming that it was under the jurisdiction of the Department of Fishes and Wildflowers, even though the rivers that run through the national forests are federal property. And just when we were getting close…" he said.

"By 'we,' he means he and Scottie," Bob interjected.

"Right. Scottie and I thought that there was more to it than just a couple seals fishing out of season to feed their families. We felt like we were starting to get close, and then we were yanked from the case. A week later, Scottie was dead. So this is personal to me now," he continued.

"Well, okay," I said. "I'll do whatever I can to help. So what's the plan? I brought my boat." I turned and pointed to the *Slayer* on its trailer. The three of us walked over to it. I could tell that Steve was not overly impressed.

"The *Myrtle*! How'd you end up with it?" he asked. "Well, it's actually Butch's, but I might buy it."

"It's not the *Myrtle* anymore. Now it's the *Steelhead Slayer*," Bob said, chuckling.

"Really. You know, Duke, it's bad luck—" Steve said before I put up my hand.

I cut him off, "I know, I know."

"Right, as long as you know," Steve said with a tone that I took as *"Don't say I didn't warn you."* Right then, the otters arrived in their huge rusty land-yacht station wagon, towing their boat. They pulled forward and then smoothly backed down the ramp until the boat floated off the trailer. Bill got out of the back seat, unhooked the boat from the trailer, and guided it to the dock, where he tied it up next to the patrol boat.

"This boat won't work, Duke," Steve said. "You won't be able to get past that first riffle at Braunschweiger Creek. It's a great boat for trolling in the bay, but pretty…um, limited upriver."

"What about if I launch at Limprock? Wouldn't three boats be better than two?" I asked. I really wanted to have the *Slayer* be part of this operation. The station wagon pulled up next to where we were standing. John, Willamina, and Dave got out.

"We ready," John said, shaking first Bob's then Steve's hand. "Hi, John. Good to see you. Thank you for coming. I appreci-ate your help," Steve said. He turned to me. "Well, okay. But hurry. You've, one, gotta get there, two, get your boat in the water, three, get your car hidden outta sight, and four, get you back to your boat fast," he said, ticking the four items off on is fingers. "Take someone with you. Willamina, you go with Duke. Hurry!"

Willamina and I sprinted to my car and sped out of the campground as fast as Prince Valiant could go—which wasn't very much. "Good morning," I said to Willamina once we were out on the main road. She had the window down and was hanging her head out of the window. I know canines like to hang out of open windows, but I never knew otters did, too.

"It stinks in here!" she shouted.

"I know. It's a surfer thing. You'll get used to it."

"Hell no, I won't! I'm not breathing that stench!"

"Well, I guess we can talk when we get to Limprock."

"If I don't pass out from holding my breath first!" she yelled back.

No other words were spoken until we had arrived at the launch ramp. Willamina jumped out of my car while it was still moving. She ran a few steps off to the side of the car. I was busy maneuvering the trailer down the slippery incline, so I lost sight of her, but I thought I heard her coughing, retching, gasping for air, or some similar sound off in the darkness.

We managed to do the four tasks that Steve had given us just as he and Bob arrived in the patrol boat. John, Bill, and Dave pulled up a few seconds behind.

"Good work, guys," Steve said. "C'mon let's get out of here before anyone shows up. We're gonna anchor up under those alders and willows over there on the south bank."

"Um…I don't have an anchor," I said sheepishly.

It was too dark to see, but I thought I heard him roll his eyes before he sighed and said, "Okay, Duke, you just tie off to John. And today, when we're done here, you go and get yourself an anchor with plenty of good stout anchor line. Basic safety equipment. Sheesh."

We motored upstream about a quarter mile and moored our boats hidden under overhanging branches. Steve and Bob were right along the bank in the patrol boat. John and his brothers were anchored right next to him, their boat covering up the reflective sides and the red-and-blue lights on the top. Willamina and I were about ten feet behind the otters' boat.

"I've been keeping in touch with a fellow Forest Circus patrolman—Cameron Haugenbeck—back at Forest Circus HQ by radio. We're using an encrypted frequency so as not to be picked up by the scanner," Steve said quietly. Voices carry over water, even more so at night it seems. "Joe and Felix would definitely have their scanners on, and probably Mike as well."

"I think I hear something," Willamina whispered just loudly enough for us all to hear.

"Okay. When I flash my lights, be ready to move. They're going to try and get away. We can corner them at the next bend upriver," Steve said softly. "Get ready to cast off your anchor lines at my mark." We all went quiet, and in a few moments, the unmistakable sound of a high-powered jet-boat could be heard approaching from the east. It was getting louder and louder as it approached. All of a sudden, a small white light, one of those pinpoint LED pencil spotlights, flashed across us.

"Now!" Steve said. Both the patrol boat's and the otter's boat's engines fired up, and the flashing red-and-blue lights from the patrol boat pierced the darkness. Willamina was on the deck in front of the windshield on my boat, reeling in the rope that had been holding us to her brothers' boat. We were drifting backward. The otters and the officers flashed powerful spotlights in the direction of the oncoming boat's engine noise. It's not easy to see a flat black boat in the dark, but I saw it veer sharply away from us, then doing a high-speed maneuver out of an old James Bond movie, whipped around 180 degrees and took off in the opposite direction. The two jet boats gunned their engines and took off in pursuit. Willamina climbed back into the cockpit of the *Slayer*, and I slammed the throttle forward. The engine sputtered, coughed, and stalled. I hit the starter, and it almost caught before going quiet again. I tried it again. Nothing. Again. Nothing. I flooded the engine, draining the battery doing so, and now we were drifting downriver toward Limprock.

"What the…?" asked Willamina. "You said Leo fixed it."

"He said he did."

"I told you, you shouldn't have renamed her," she said.

I pulled out the water ski and paddling, used it to get us to the boat ramp.

"Nice paddle," she quipped as we tied up to the little dock. "Now what, Einstein?"

I moved closer to her and whispered, "Don't look now, but I think we've got company." I could see headlights flashing through the trees as a vehicle approached. I untied the *Slayer* and pushed her out into the current. She spun lazily and started drifting downriver.

"What are you *doing?*" Willamina hissed.

"They know this boat. It can't be here," I said. "C'mon, let's get outta sight."

We ran off the dock and hid in the scratchberry bushes off to the side as the same phone company truck that we've been chasing backed down the ramp. About ten yards after it went past us, it stopped. The headlights were turned off, and the front doors opened. Out climbed Mike Wilson and Felix, the ranger. We ducked down into the bushes further. Wilson lit a cigarette and walked to the back of the truck, looking out across the dark still water, talking on a cell phone. The ranger met him there and lit one up himself.

"Well, they're late," Felix said. "That's not like them."

Wilson hung up his phone. "There was a voice mail from the downstream team. They didn't catch enough to make it worth wasting the gas. They're not coming at all."

"Yeah, the catches have been getting smaller and smaller. This is probably our last load, and I think we're gonna lose money on it, too."

"Right, we've been just breaking even these past few days," Wilson said. "Time to cut and run."

While they were talking, Willamina and I slowly and quietly climbed out of the scratchberry bushes and started sneaking in the opposite direction. We hadn't gotten more than a few silent steps away when suddenly two headlights and a bright spotlight shone brightly in our faces, freezing us in our tracks. Flashing red-and-blue lights started spinning above the spotlight. The driver's door of the squad car opened, and a familiar voice shouted, "Stay right there, Hazzard!"

It was Joe Wilson's voice. Willamina and I stood there stiffly for a second and slowly turned toward each other. The look in her eyes was pure fury—it scared the bejesus out of me. I didn't know who I should be more afraid of—her or the corrupt giant of a cop. As I was looking at her, I saw a large pair of hands come from behind and grab her upper arms. At the same time, I felt two hands like iron clamps close down on my biceps.

"Turn off those freaking lights, you idiot!" Mike Wilson, who was holding Willamina, yelled at his brother. "How stupid *are* you?" In a hummingbird heartbeat, the lights went out. In the sudden darkness, I couldn't see a thing, but I couldn't move either. Joe came up behind us and handcuffed each of us. He and his brother escorted us to his car, where we were roughly shoved into the back scat—Willamina behind the driver's seat, me behind the passenger's seat. There was a passenger up front. It was Judy Boodles.

"Okay, I guess these two are throwing a little wrench in our plans," Mike, obviously the guy in charge, said. "Take them down to Dogstown and toss them in the clink."

"What about her?" Joe asked, nodding in the direction of Judy in the front seat.

Mike said, "Take her, too. Throw her in a different cell. Charge her with being an accessory to murder. We'll pin that on one of the seals. We'll tell everyone she was the mastermind of this whole operation. Gives us time to get away—after this one last load. Let her rich daddy buy her way out," He paused, and it was quiet in the predawn. "Get going. I can hear the upstream boat coming."

Joe climbed back into his cop car and started out of the campground.

Just as we were leaving the campground and turning onto the main road, a green Forest Circus SUV with lights flashing squealed to a stop, blocking our way. The driver got out and pointed his spotlight into the cockpit of our car. He said something into the microphone pinned to his Kevlar vest. As he was speaking, another county sheriff 's car pulled in—its lights flashing as well—and also shone his spotlight directly at us. Joe—not to be outdone—turned on his flashers as well. It was quite the light show, with red-and-blue strobe lights reflecting off of the dew-wetted fall foliage. Joe got out of our car, and Ursalik lumbered out of the other county car.

Over the loudspeaker, Ursalik's voice boomed, "Hold it right there, Wilson!" Put your hands up where I can see 'em and get away from the car."

We were blinded by the dual spotlights, so we couldn't see if there were guns pointed at Joe or not, and I'll bet dog biscuits to dollars that Joe couldn't see, either. So in one of the more intelligent moves I've seen the dog do, he raised his hands and moved a couple feet to his left. He squinted into the lights. "But, Captain, I've got the otter murderer and his accomplices right here. Hazzard killed the otter. Boodles is the brains of the outfit!" He lowered his right arm and pointed at the three of us in the car. "She and her seal friends have been illegally catching fish and selling them to muskrats for their lutefisk factories in Canadia. They hired Hazzard for '*protection*.'"

It wasn't quite the story that his brother had laid out, but it was close.

"Put your hand back up, Wilson! Is that you in there, Hazzard?" the ol' grizzly growled. "Haugenbeck, keep Wilson covered. Hazzard, get out of the car with your hands up!"

"No, I can't!" I shouted back. "What! You get out right now!"

"I'm handcuffed, and the doors are locked from the outside!"

"Oh, for Pete's sake…" Ursalik walked over and yanked the door open, reached in, grabbed me by the scruff of the neck, and threw me out onto the sharp crushed gravel shoulder. I landed on my shoulder and smacked my chin into the stones. He left the back door open and looked through the front passenger's window. Opening the front door, he said, "I *thought* that was you, Miss Boodles. What *are* you doing here?"

She remained facing forward with her eyes closed in the glare of the spotlights. Quietly she said, "I am innocent, Captain. Wilson said my father wanted me to meet someone here, so I came with him. I don't know anything about stealing fish and even less about a murdered otter."

"She's the mastermind of the whole operation, Captain!" Wilson shouted.

"Shut up, Wilson!" Ursalik barked back. "Please get out of the car, Ms. Boodles." Looking in the back seat, he said, "Who are *you*?

"Willamina Illahe."

"Outta the car, Ms. Illahe," Ursalik said. "I can't. Handcuffs. Door locked."

"Please slide your little derriere over, across the seat, and get out," he said politely before shouting, "Now!"

Willamina sighed and moved over, swung her lovely legs out, and stood up in front of Ursalik. "Okay. I'm out. Happy now?"

By this time, I had managed to sit upright with my legs stretched out in front of me. My face hurt where it hit the rocks, and I could see blood dripping onto my jeans.

"Sit down next to him," he said to her while glaring at me. "Up. Down. Up. Down," she said as she sat at my side.

"I know you don't like cops, but please be nice," I whispered. "*Don't like? I hate* cops," she spat back just loud enough for Ursalik to hear.

"We're not in a very strong bargaining position right now," I continued to whisper.

Willamina just gritted her teeth, frowned, and stared forward, chin raised and eyes sparkling with fury. In the pink glow of the sunrise, I thought she was the most beautiful creature I had ever seen.

Angry but gorgeous. Even if she *was* going to get me thrown in jail. "Captain, look. Here comes somebody," Haugenbeck's voice came from behind the glare. The sky continued to lighten. Walking up the road—still about a hundred yards away—were three seals with their hands handcuffed behind their backs. Behind them were Mike Wilson and Felix, the ranger, with their zip-tied hands in the air. Behind them were Bob and Steve, with their guns pointed at the procession in front of them.

While Willamina, Ursalik, and the rest of us were having our little meeting up by the road, here's what happened down at the river. The black boat came around the last upstream bend and pulled up to the small floating dock at the boat ramp.

Mike flashed his flashlight at the boat and saw Steve at the helm and Bob standing behind the windshield. Both had their revolvers drawn and pointing at Mike and Felix. Three seals were sitting in the stern of the boat in handcuffs and trussed up together in the anchor line like a Sunday goose.

"Hold it right there, Wilson. You too, Felix," Steve shouted authoritatively.

Bob lashed the boat to the dock. He and Steve walked up the ramp and using zip-ties, cuffed the two with their hands in front of them.

"Okay, Felix, turn around and lean against the truck face first. Wilson, you turn around and lean up against him." Both men did as they were told. "Bob, if they move, shoot. With that hand canon you've got, one bullet is all you need. Your first shot will go right through Wilson and into Felix."

"Got it," Bob said.

"Rest easy, boys, I'm going to get your seal buddies, and then we're gonna have a little parade.

"Now what the hell do we have?" Ursalik growled. "Dispatch? Ursalik here. Send the Black Maria up to Limprock Campground."

"Black Maria?" a voice crackled over the PA system

"The paddy wagon! You know, the 'Secure Multi-Prisoner Transport Vehicle!'" Ursalik shouted into his phone. "We've got"—

he paused, and I could see his lips move as he counted with his eyes—"at least eight prisoners to take in."

"10-4, Captain," the crackly voice continued. "Roger that. Out." Ursalik rolled his eyes and breathed a deep sigh. By this time, the prisoner parade had arrived.

"There she is! That's her! Arrest her! Judy Boodles hired the seals to kill that otter. That cat is in on it, too! He's running the salmon poaching operation for her!" shouted Mike Wilson.

"Whoever you are, shut the hell up! Maypox! What is going on here?" snarled an exasperated Ursalik. Is that your brother, Wilson?" he asked Joe.

"Yes," Mike and Joe Wilson answered simultaneously. I had heard that twins often do stuff like that, but to experience it in real life was kinda weird.

"Well, it's a long story, Captain. You see, Duke there came to me with some evidence that—" Bob started before Ursalik cut him off, holding an island-sized hand palm forward at him.

"Stop. Just stop," he said. "Bottom-line it for me, Maypox. Who killed the otter?"

"He did! The ranger cat did it," shouted one of the seals. "He borrowed our boat. Said he was going fishing. The next morning Scottie was dead and there was blood in our boat."

"It was fish blood!" Felix countered. "Right? I told you that."

"No, you said, 'If anyone asks, that's *fish* blood.' That's what you said," the seal replied. "You didn't catch no fish. You caught an otter messing with our nets. And you killed him."

"Okay, so maybc I did kill him, but it was her dad that ordered it." He pointed at Judy Boodles.

EPILOGUE

Willamina finally agreed to accompany me to Swindler's but only under the condition that I restore *Myrtle* to her proper name before we go.

Over cocktails while waiting to order our dinners, I said, "Here you go." I held up my cell phone so she could see a photo—my very first phone photo—of the transom of *Myrtle* with her name repainted in large pink letters. "Proof."

"You're lucky my brothers went looking for her when you sent her off downriver. They didn't know what happened to us."

"Yeah. It got a little scraped up, and I definitely need a new prop now." I laughed.

"So it was Judy Boodles's dad?" she asked.

"Yeah. As it turns out, Steve, was at one point, trying to catch the gillnetting seals. However, it started to get a little deeper, more than just some seals stealing salmon. Steve was on to the whole process. It turned into a murder with the death of Scottie. But somehow before then, he was pulled off the case, and it was assigned to the Department of Fishes and Wildflowers. Apparently the state thought it was under their jurisdiction, it wasn't a federal matter. Aris Boodles—Judy's dad—is one of the civilians appointed by the gov-ernor to be on the DFW Board of Commissioners. He's got money, and he's got connected friends. He arranged to have Ranger Felix be the one assigned to the case. Felix and the Wilsons put up roadblocks to keep people away. Scottie was helping out Steve, but had gotten a bit drunk and started mouthing off at the Poison Oak when Steve got pulled off the case. The seal gang was there, and the leader of the seal gang told their boss, Felix, about what they had heard."

"I heard about that," Willamina said. "I was off that night."

"Through the urging of Felix and Joe Wilson, Ursalik quickly and easily turned it around into a high-profile boating accident, keeping even more people off the river at night, making it easier for them to gillnet without getting caught."

"Have I told you I don't like cops?" she asked jokingly.

"Old man Boodles also arranged to have his daughter assigned to the newly created city manager job, with Joe Wilson hired to be her bodyguard, so he had two people on the inside, plus Felix."

The waiter approached and said, "Good evening and welcome to Swindler's. Tonight's special is poached salmon."

www.ingramcontent.com/pod-product-compliance
Lightning Source LLC
Chambersburg PA
CBHW040830010826
48978CB00012BB/687